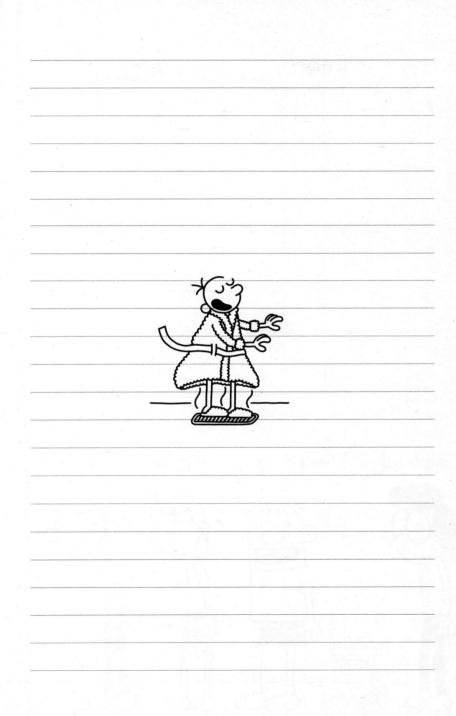

DIARY
of a Wimpy Kid

小屁孩日记⑤

——午餐零食大盗

[美]杰夫·金尼　著

陈万如　译

格雷的老爸

格雷

·广州·

广东省出版集团

新世纪出版社

本书简体中文版由美国 Harry N. Abrams 公司通过中国 Creative Excellence Rights Agency 独家授权

版权合同登记号：19-2010-050 号

图书在版编目（CIP）数据

小屁孩日记⑤：午餐零食大盗/〔美〕杰夫·金尼著；

陈万如译. —广州：新世纪出版社，2010.7（2011.10 重印）

ISBN 978-7-5405-4350-1

Ⅰ. 小… Ⅱ.①杰… ②陈… Ⅲ. 日记体小说-美国-现代

Ⅳ. I712.45

中国版本图书馆 CIP 数据核字（2009）第 200727 号

出 版 人：孙泽军
选题策划：王小斌
责任编辑：王小斌 傅 琨
责任技编：王建慧

小屁孩日记⑤
——午餐零食大盗

〔美〕 杰夫·金尼 著 陈万如 译

出版发行：新世纪出版社
经 销：全国新华书店
印 刷：广东省教育厅教育印刷厂
开 本：890mm×1240mm 1/32
印 张：6.75 字 数：130 千字
版 次：2010 年 7 月第 1 版
印 次：2011 年 10 月第 8 次印刷
印 数：105 001～115 000
书 号：ISBN 978-7-5405-4350-1
定 价：14.90 元

质量监督电话：020-83797655 购书咨询电话：020-83781545

"小屁孩之父" 杰夫·金尼致中国粉丝

中国的"哈屁族":

你们好!

从小我就对中国很着迷,现在能给中国读者写信真是我的荣幸啊。我从来没想过自己会成为作家,更没想到我的作品会流传到你们的国家,一个离我家十万八千里的地方。

当我还是个小屁孩的时候,我和我的朋友曾试着挖地洞,希望一直挖下去就能到地球另一端的中国。不一会儿,我们就放弃了这个想法(要知道,挖洞是件多辛苦的事儿啊!);但现在通过我的这些作品,我终于到中国来了——只是通过另一种方式,跟我的想象有点不一样的方式。

谢谢你们让《小屁孩日记》在中国成为畅销书。我希望你们觉得这些故事是有趣的,也希望这些故事对你们是一种激励,让你们有朝一日也成为作家和漫画家。我是幸运的,因为我的梦想就是成为一个漫画家,而现在这个梦想实现了。不管你们的梦想是什么,我都希望你们梦想成真。

我希望有朝一日能亲身到中国看看。这是个将要实现的梦想!

希望你们喜欢《小屁孩日记》的第五册(编者注:即中译本第9、10册)。再次感谢你们对这套书的喜爱!

杰夫

A Letter to Chinese Readers

Hello to all my fans in China!

I've had a fascination with China ever since I was a boy, and it's a real privilege to be writing to you now. I never could have imagined that I would become an author, and that my work would reach a place as far from my home as your own country.

When I was a kid, my friends and I tried to dig a hole in the ground, because we hoped we could reach China on the other side of the earth. We gave up after a few minutes (digging is hard!), but with these books, I'm getting to reach your country... just in a different way than I had imagined.

Thank you so much for making **Diary of a Wimpy Kid** a success in your country. I hope you find the stories funny and that they inspire you to become writers and cartoonists. I feel very fortunate to have achieved my dream to become a cartoonist, and I hope you achieve your dream, too... whatever it might be.

I hope to one day visit China. It would be a dream come true!

I hope you enjoy the fifth **Wimpy Kid** book. Thank you again for embracing my books!

Jeff

有趣的书，好玩的书

夏致

这是一个美国中学男生的日记。他为自己的瘦小个子而苦恼，老是会担心被同班的大块头欺负，会感慨"为什么分班不是按个头分而是按年龄分"。这是他心里一道小小的自卑，可是另一方面呢，他又为自己的脑瓜比别人灵光而沾沾自喜，心里嘲笑同班同学是笨蛋，老想投机取巧偷懒。

他在老妈的要求下写日记，幻想着自己成名后拿日记本应付蜂拥而至的记者；他特意在分班时装得不会念书，好让自己被分进基础班，打的主意是"尽可能降低别人对你的期望值，这样即使最后你可能几乎什么都不用干，也总能给他们带来惊喜"；他喜欢玩电子游戏，可是他爸爸常常把他赶出家去，好让他多活动一下。结果他跑到朋友家里去继续打游戏，然后在回家的路上用别人家的喷水器弄湿身子，扮成一身大汗的样子；他眼红自己的好朋友手受伤以后得到女生的百般呵护，就故意用绷带把自己的手掌缠得严严实实的装伤员，没招来女生的关注反而惹来自己不想搭理的人；不过，一山还有一山高，格雷再聪明，在家里还是敌不过哥哥罗德里克，还是被耍得团团转；而正在上幼儿园的弟弟曼尼可以"恃小卖小"，无论怎么捣蛋都有爸妈护着，让格雷无可奈何。

这个狡黠、机趣、自恋、胆小、爱出风头、喜欢懒散的男孩，一点都不符合人们心目中的那种懂事上进的好孩子形象，奇怪的是这个缺点不少的男孩子让我忍不住喜欢他。

人们总想对生活中的一切事情贴上个"好"或"坏"的标签。要是找不出它的实在可见的好处，它就一定是"坏"，是没有价值的。单纯的有趣，让我们增添几分好感和热爱，这难道不是比读书学习考试重要得多的事情吗?! 生活就像一个蜜糖罐子，我们是趴在桌子边踮高脚尖伸出手，眼巴巴地瞅着罐子的孩子。有趣不就是蜂蜜的滋味吗?

翻开这本书后，我每次笑声与下一次笑声之间停顿不超过五分钟。一是因为格雷满脑子的鬼主意和诡辩，实在让人忍俊不禁。二是因为我还能毫不费劲地明白他的想法，一下子就捕捉到格雷的逻辑好笑在哪里，然后会心一笑。

小学二年级的时候我和同班的男生打架；初一的时候放学后我在黑板上写"某某某（男生）是个大笨蛋"；初二的时候，同桌的男生起立回答老师的提问，我偷偷移开他的椅子，让他的屁股结结实实地亲吻了地面……我对初中男生的记忆少得可怜。到了高中，进了一所重点中学，大多数的男生要么是专心学习的乖男孩，要么是个性飞扬的早熟少年。除了愚人节和邻班的同学集体调换教室糊弄老师以外，男生们很少再玩恶作剧了。仿佛大家不约而同都知道，自己已经过了有资格耍小聪明，并且耍完以后别人会觉得自己可爱的年龄了。

如果你是一位超过中学年龄的大朋友，欢迎你和我在阅读时光中做一次短暂的童年之旅；如果你是格雷的同龄人，我真羡慕你们，因为你们读了这本日记之后，还可以在自己的周围发现比格雷的经历更妙趣横生的小故事，让阅读的美好体验延续到生活里。

要是给我一个机会再过一次童年，我一定会睁大自己还没有患上近视的眼睛，仔细发掘身边有趣的小事情，拿起笔记录下来。亲爱的读者，不知道当你读完这本小书后，是否也有同样的感觉?

片刻之后我转念一想，也许从现在开始，还来得及呢。作者创作这本图画日记那年是 30 岁，那么说来我还有 9 年时间呢。

一月

元旦

你知道，每到年初，无论如何你都得立下一个新年誓愿，好督促自己争取进步。

问题是，要我想出办法来完善自己可真不容易，因为我是我认识的人当中最优秀的。

所以今年我的誓愿是努力帮助别人进步。但我发现有些人并不领我的情。

很快我就注意到，家里其他人都不怎么把新年誓愿当回事。

老妈之前说她今天要开始上健身房，可她整个下午都在看电视。

老爸说他要严格控制饮食，可晚饭后他在车库里把嘴巴塞满了巧克力饼干，被我逮个正着。

就连我的小·弟曼尼，也践行不了自己的新年誓愿。

今天早上他跟每个人都说他是"大男孩"了，要和安慰奶嘴永远告别。说完他把最心爱的奶嘴扔进垃圾桶里。

结果，这个新年誓愿持续不到一分钟就完蛋了。

家里没有立下新年誓愿的只有我哥罗德里克一个。那太可惜了，按理来说他的誓愿得排成一张2400米长的清单。

于是我决定想个办法帮助罗德里克提高素质。我把这个计划叫做"三振出局"①。大意是每回我看到罗德里克捣乱，就在他的计划表格上画个小小的"×"。

但我还没来得及想好"出局"代表什么意思，罗德里克就用完三次的限额了。

① 这句话出自棒球比赛的规则，击球手三次挥棒没有击中对方的投球就出局。译者注

不管怎么说，我开始考虑是不是也要把我的誓愿搁置起来。帮助别人进步很费功夫，而且到现在还没什么进展。

另外，在我第一百万次提醒老妈吃薯片别嚼那么大声之后，她提出一个非常好的理由。她说，"格雷，不是每个人都可以像你这么完美的。"根据我一向的观察所得，她说得对。

周四

老爸又一次节食，对我来说这是个坏消息。他已经连续三天不沾一点巧克力，人变得超级不可理喻。

前几天，老爸叫我起床准备上学，我不知不觉又睡着了。你相信我吧，我以后再也不会犯那样的错误了。

出问题的一部分原因是老爸总是不等老妈洗完澡①就叫我起床，所以我知道实际上我可以在床上多躺十几分钟再起来。

昨天我想到一个既能多睡一会儿又不会惹老爸发火的办法。做法是他叫我起床后，我带齐被子、毛毯到客厅，在洗手间外面等着老妈出来。

然后我可以躺在暖气出口的正上方。暖气一烧起来，躺在那里比躺在床上还舒服。

问题是，暖气一次只持续五分钟。暖气一停下来，我就躺在冰冷的金属片上。

今天早上，我在等着老妈洗完澡，突然记起来圣诞节时有人送了一件浴袍给她。于是我翻开她的衣橱拿出浴袍。

我一点也不夸张地说，这是我有史以来最英明的举动之一。穿着那玩意，就像裹在一条刚烘干的松软的大毛巾里。

说真的，我对这件浴袍喜欢得不得了，洗完澡之后继续穿。我觉得老爸因为自己没想起有件浴袍而妒忌我，因为今天我走到餐桌时，老爸看起来老大不高兴。

早上好！

我跟你说，女人想出穿浴袍的主意真不错。现在我琢磨着还有什么东西我没想起来。

我真希望之前圣诞节的时候我要的礼物是浴袍，因为我肯定老妈会叫我还她浴袍。

今年我又栽在礼物上面了。圣诞节早上下了楼，看到我那只长筒袜里只有一支除臭剂和一本《旅行指南》，我就知道这一天算是完了。

　　我猜，一旦你进了中学，大人们就觉得你已经过了享用玩具和有趣小·玩意的年龄了。

　　可他们依然期待你在拆开那些没意思的礼物时会欢呼雀跃。

　　数学真有趣

今年我收到的大部分礼物都是书本或者衣服。看起来最接近玩具的是查理叔叔的礼物。

打开查理叔叔的礼物时，我居然认不出那是啥。一个大大的塑料环，上面套着一个网兜。

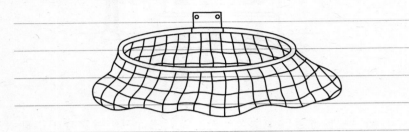

查理叔叔解释那是个放在卧室的脏衣袋。他说袋子要挂在门后，这样我放脏衣服进去就成一件乐事了。

起初我以为他在开玩笑，然而不久以后我意识到查理叔叔是认真的。我得跟他解释我其实不用自己洗衣服。

我告诉他，我只管把脏衣服丢在地板上，老妈自然会把衣服捡起来，拿到楼下的洗衣间洗。

几天后，衣服就会干干净净、整整齐齐地回到我的房间里。

我跟查理叔叔说，他应该收回这个洗衣袋，给我兑成现金，让我买些自己用得上的东西。

这时候老妈开腔了。她对查理叔叔说，她觉得送脏衣袋的点子真不错。然后她说，从今以后我得自己洗衣服。这等于是说，圣诞节查理叔叔送了我一件家务活。

今年我净是收到这么些差劲的礼物，真让人不爽。之前的几个月我用尽十八般武艺去讨大人欢心，满以为圣诞节的时候我的努力会得到回报。

现在我得自己洗衣服。我挺庆幸收到的礼物中有好几件衣服，因此可能我整个学年都有足够的干净衣服穿了。

周一

今天我和罗利去车站坐车，意外得知一个讨厌的消息。有张纸贴在路牌上，说"公交线路重新安排，此站取消，即日生效"。那就是说从现在起我们得走路上学。

　　这下，我想跟出这个主意的聪明人谈一谈，因为我们住的街离学校差不多有四百米的距离。

　　我和罗利今天得跑步上学才能不迟到。让人气急败坏的是我们平日坐的公交车从我们身边驶过，车上满载着住在我家相邻的威利街的小·孩。

　　车子驶过我们身边时，威利街的小·孩在学猴子叫。以前我们坐车从他们身边经过时，就是这么做的。气死我了！

我告诉你让小·孩走路上学不好的一个原因。这些天老师布置那么多作业，你的书包里装着要带回家的书本和试卷，背起来就像一块大石头。

要是你想知道长期负重会对小·孩有什么影响，你只要看一下罗德里克和他的几个朋友就行了。

老爸今天和小·流氓干了漂亮的一仗。我们街区最痞的小·流氓是一个叫兰伍德·希斯的小·孩，他有点像是老爸的天敌。老爸大概已经给警察打过50次电话举报兰伍德·希斯了。

我猜兰伍德的父母烦透他了，因为他们要送他到军事学院。

你大概会以为兰伍德去了军校会让老爸挺高兴的。不过我觉得，除非这个星球上每个小·流氓都被送去少年管教所或者阿尔卡特兹监狱①，否则老爸都不会满意。罗德里克也应在遣送对象之列。

昨天老妈老爸给罗德里克一些钱，让他去买书准备SAT考试，可罗德里克却把钱用来做了刺青。

水不湿②

我可能还有一小·段时间才会变成小·流氓。不过我敢保证，我一踏入小·流氓的行列，老爸就会时刻寻找机会把我遣送出去。

星期一

上个星期曼尼每天晚上都从床上爬起来，走下楼。

老妈没把他哄回床上去，反而让他和我们坐在一起看电视。

真不公平，曼尼和我们在一起的时候，老妈就不给我看我喜欢的节目。

① 以前美国一个小岛上的监狱，以防卫严密、极难越狱而闻名。译者注
② 罗德里克的乐队名称，详见《小屁孩日记1》。译者注

同人不同命。我小时候可完全没有得到这种"晚上下床"的待遇。有一两回我下床了，不过老爸很快就阻止了我。

那时候老爸每晚都给我念一本叫《爱心树》的故事书。那确实是本好书，书的封底是作者的照片，这个家伙叫谢尔·希尔弗斯坦。

可是，谢尔·希尔弗斯坦长得根本不像一个儿童故事书的作者，而像一个入室大盗。

老爸准是知道那张照片有点吓到了我，有天晚上我从床上爬下来，老爸说：

要是你今晚再下床，你说不定就会在走廊上遇见谢尔·希尔弗斯坦。

这招一试就灵。从那时起直到现在，哪怕半夜我真的很想上厕所，我也不会下床。

我认为老爸老妈没有给曼尼念过谢尔·希尔弗斯坦的书，这很可能是为什么他们哄曼尼睡觉后曼尼总是会下床。

我听过老妈老爸给曼尼念的几个故事，请允许我这么说：那些写书的人真的是在骗小·孩。

首先，书里几乎没有多少文字，我敢肯定五秒钟就能写一本这样的书来。

笨熊打哈欠，笨熊悲伤。笨熊正睡觉，笨熊喜洋洋！完了。

我把自己对曼尼的故事书的看法告诉老妈，她说要是那些书那么容易就能写出来，我应该自己写一本试试。

我真的听老妈的话写了一本。相信我吧，那也不难。你要做的就是给主角起一个朗朗上口的名字，然后确保主角在故事结束的时候接受一个教训。

现在我需要做的就是把这份东西寄给一家出版社，然后就等着钞票滚滚来。

别傻了，施若夏普先生！

作者：格雷·赫夫利

从前有个男人叫施若夏普先生，他脑袋里总有一些疯狂的想法。

我知道的事情不多，但有一件事我知道：北极熊这种动物毫无用处。

有一天施若夏普先生驾着自己的小车到外面溜达。

我来了……

然而……

哎呀！

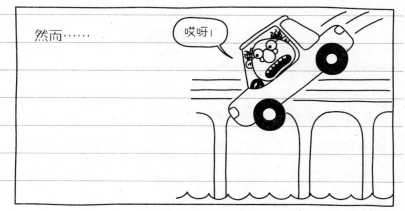

然后……

所以呢……

故事终。

　　知道我刚才说的是什么意思吧？完工以后我注意到，唯一一个缺陷是我忘了把字句写成押韵的。不过要是出版社想要押韵，他们得多付我点钱。

周六

连续两周走路上学，我无比期待周末两天能舒舒服服、无所事事地在家歇着。

问题来了。周六的电视节目，要么是保龄球，要么是高尔夫球。而且阳光从侧面的滑动玻璃窗照射进来，你基本上看不清电视屏幕。

今天我想换个频道，可是遥控器在咖啡桌上。我已经非常舒服地坐着了，一碗燕麦粥搁在膝上，真不想站起来。

尽管过去无数次尝试没一次成功，我还是努力用意念让遥控器朝我腾空飞来。今天我尝试了十五分钟，调动了全部注意力，不过依然不走运。我真希望我能够知道这十五分钟老爸一直站在我身后。

　　老爸跟我说，我得到户外锻炼一下。我跟他说我一直都在锻炼，今天早上我还用了他送我的推举器。

　　我本来该找一段更可信的台词。很显然我没有真的去做推举练习。

知道吗？老爸总是在运动锻炼这些事情上找我的茬，那是因为他有个叫沃伦先生的上司。沃伦先生有三个儿子，个个都是运动狂人。每天老爸和别人拼车下班回家，经过沃伦家时总能看到沃伦家的小孩在草坪上运动。

　　我想老爸每次回家看到自己的三个儿子在干啥的时候，心里一定相当失望。

不管怎么样，就像我说的，今天老爸就把我赶到屋外。我真的想不到有什么运动是我想做的，不过随后我想出一个好主意。

昨天午饭时，阿尔伯特·萨迪跟每个人喋喋不休地谈论这个不知是在中国还是泰国的家伙，说他可以往上一跃，直直地跳到六尺高的空中，一点不假。这家伙可以在地上挖个三英寸深的洞，来回跳进跳出一百次。

第二天，这家伙把洞挖深一倍，继续反复跳进跳出。到了第五天，他几乎成了一只袋鼠。

我那一桌有几个家伙说阿尔伯特在胡说八道。不过我觉得他说的很有道理。还有，我考虑过我要是按照他所说的来做，再把训练时间延长几天，我受欺负的事就一下子成为过去时。

我从车库里拿出一把铲子，在前院找到一个看上去挺适合挖洞的地方。可我还没来得及动手，老妈就出来质问我要干吗。

我告诉老妈我只是在挖个洞，当然她不会喜欢我这个想法。于是她提出了二十个左右的理由说明为什么不许我挖洞。

　　老妈跟我说，在院子挖洞"危险"，因为地下布有电线和排污管等等。然后她翻来覆去让我答应不会在院子里挖洞。我答应了。

　　老妈走进屋里，但她之后一直透过窗子盯着我。我知道我得带着铲子到别的地方去了。于是我直奔罗利家。

　　最近我没怎么去罗利家，主要是因为弗雷格。弗雷格这些天长时间呆在他家院子里。果不其然，今天他也在那里。

这块痂闻起来好玩吗？

　　我对弗雷格的新招是避免和他有眼神接触，径直往前走。今天这招看起来很管用。

到罗利家后，我跟他说了挖洞的事，还告诉他如果我们坚持按我的计划来跳洞，我们两个人就能成为日本武士那样的人物。

可罗利看起来不大热衷这件事。他说要是我们没跟他爸妈打招呼，就在他家前院挖一个十英尺深的洞，他们可能会气得发狂，所以他得先请求爸妈的批准。

现在，如果要说我对罗利的爸妈有一点了解的话，那就是他们从来不喜欢我的想法。我告诉罗利我们可以用一块防水布或者毯子之类的东西盖住洞口，上面再铺些树叶，他爸妈就永远不会发现这个洞。这个说法似乎说服了罗利。

我承认罗利的父母最终还是会发现的，行了吧。可这种情况至少得过三四个月才会发生。

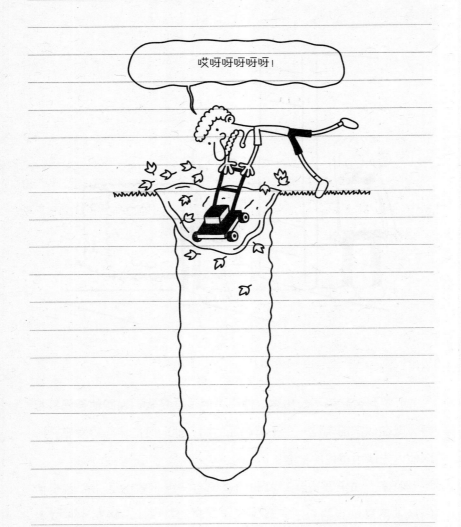

　　我和罗利在前院找到一个好地方，开始挖洞，但我们马上碰到钉子了。

地面冻得硬邦邦的，我们连个凹洞都挖不出来。

咯噔

我奋斗了好几分钟，才把铲子递给罗利。他也没取得什么进展。不过我让他干了很长时间才接手，好让他感觉到他为这个项目贡献良多。

小口喝热水

挖

罗利比我稍微能干一点，但天黑下来的时候，他还是放弃了。

估计明天我们得换个法子干这事。

周日

　　喏，为了这件事我昨晚绞尽脑汁，然后我意识到照现在的进度，等这个洞挖到十英尺深，我和罗利都要上大学了。

　　于是我产生了一个截然不同的想法。我记得在电视上看过，科学家造了一个"时光宝盒"，往里面放了一堆东西，像报纸、DVD光盘之类的，然后把时光宝盒埋在地下。科学家的设想是几百年后有人会来到那个地方，把东西挖出来，他们就可以知道我们是怎样生活的了。

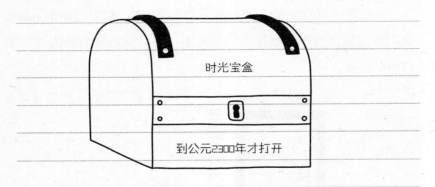

时光宝盒

到公元2300年才打开

　　我把想法告诉罗利，看起来他对这个想法充满热情。我觉得他之所以高兴是因为我们不用把接下来的几年时间都花在挖洞上。

　　我叫罗利捐出一些东西放在时光宝盒里，这时候他想退缩了。

　　我告诉罗利，要是他往时光宝盒里放些自己的圣诞节礼物，未来的人打开盒子后就会大有所获。罗利跟我说这不公平，因为我也没有把自己的圣诞礼物放进时光宝盒。于是我不得不跟他解释，如果未来的人打开盒子，发现里面全是衣服和书，他们会觉得我们非常没劲。

　　然后我告诉罗利我会从自己的积蓄中掏三美元放进盒子里，来证明我也有所牺牲。看起来这样子足以说服罗利交出一盘新游戏碟和其他几样什么东西。

　　其实我有一个秘密想法没透露给罗利。我知道往时光宝盒里放钞票是个英明的举动，因为到将来那张钞票的价值会远远超过三美元。

　　希望找到时光宝盒的人会穿越时空回来，报答我让他们发了财。

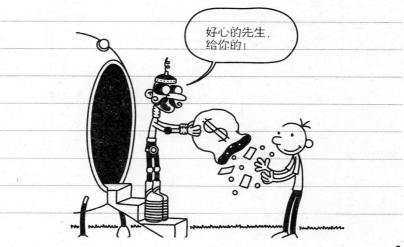

好心的先生，
给你的！

我写了一张小·便笺，放进盒子里，以确保找到盒子的人可以清楚知道他要感谢的人是谁。

致启者：
这些钞票的捐出者是
格雷·赫夫利
萨里大街12号

　　我和罗利找到一个鞋盒，把我们的东西全放了进去。然后我们用防护胶带给鞋盒封口。

　　我在盒子外面写了留言，确保人们不会太早打开它。

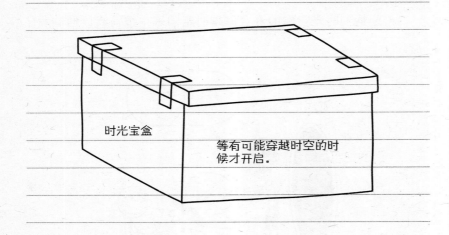

时光宝盒

等有可能穿越时空的时候才开启。

然后我们把盒子放进我们昨天挖好的洞里，尽可能把它埋好。

　　要是罗利之前挖洞多卖力一点就好了，因为我们的时光宝盒不能整个埋在地下。但愿没人会破坏它，它至少得在那里呆好几百年呢。

拍拍

周一

　　唉，我这个星期打一开始就过得不顺。往常老妈的浴袍会挂在我房门的把手上，今天起床后我发现它不见了。

　　我问老妈是不是她拿回去了，可她说没有。我有种预感：老爸对它动了手脚。

　　几天前，我想出一个办法把浴袍和暖气口的享受结合起来，我觉得老爸一点也不喜欢我的点子。

啊！

呼噜

　　我觉得他要么是把浴袍藏起来了，要么是把它扔了。我想起来了！老爸昨天晚饭后跑去慈善中心，这十有八九不是什么好北头。

　　话说回来，要是老爸真的扔了浴袍，那也不是他第一回扔掉别人的个人财物。你知道曼尼一直以来怎么样挣扎着戒掉他的安慰奶嘴吗？

　　昨天早上老爸把曼尼的奶嘴扔了个精光，一个不落。

　　这下，曼尼彻底抓狂了。老妈能摆平他的唯一办法是翻出他的旧毯子，他管这东西叫"小·可爱"。

　　"小·可爱"本是老妈在曼尼一岁生日时织给他的蓝色小毯，曼尼对它一见钟情。

　　曼尼到哪里都带着它，和它形影不离，甚至不让老妈拿去清洗。

毯子开始走形了，到曼尼两岁的时候，毯子基本上就成了由葡萄干和鼻屎粘连起来的几根纱线。

我想曼尼就在那个时候起开始管他的毯子叫"小·可爱"的。

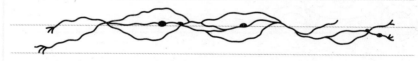

这几天，曼尼一直拖着"小·可爱"满房子走，就像他孩提时候那样。我一直尽力给他让路。

周三

　　每天走路上学累得我够呛，今天早上我问老妈能不能载我和罗利上学。之前我没问她，是因为老妈车子的保险杠上贴满那些囧得要命的贴纸。对这类东西我们学校的小孩会毫不留情。

　　我试着撕下贴纸，但粘贴纸的胶水质量太好了，一粘上去，万年不掉。

我的孩子毕业于
温柔抚育
幼儿班

　　今天我和罗利搭了老妈的车，不过我叫她在学校后面停车，让我们下来。

你确定就在这里下车吗？

对，谢谢司机！

哎，我笨死了，居然把书包忘在车里。老妈在第四节课捎书包给我，当然她终于在今天开始去健身了。

宝宝，你忘了拿书包！

这只能算在我的运气头上。我只有第四节课和荷莉·希尔斯一起上，今年我一直努力给她留下个好印象。恐怕这次我的进度要倒退三周了。

我也不是唯一一个卖力吸引荷莉·希尔斯的人。我想在班上每个男生都在暗恋她。

论漂亮荷莉在班上排第四，但前三甲都名花有主了。很多人像我一样，要尽法宝想和她交往。

我一直在想用什么办法能把自己和其他喜欢荷莉的愣头青区别开来，最后我终于想到了：幽默感。

知道吧，在幽默感方面班上的小孩就像原始人。为了让你们对我说的话有个形象的理解，下面就是每天学校里流传的段子——

不论什么时候，只要荷莉在我附近，我一定有多好表现多好。

最近我一直让罗利做我的相声搭档，我也确实训练罗利表演了好几个挺有内涵的笑话。

唯一的问题是，罗利开始和我争谁该说哪句台词，我不知道这种搭档关系能不能长期维持下去。

罗利："小·狗丢下来的"那句让我来说行不行？

格雷：唔……我觉得那样不好。

周五

哎，坐老妈的车上学我得到教训了，于是我又改回走路。不过今天下午和罗利一起放学回家，我严重地意识到我没力气爬上山回自家的屋子。于是我问罗利能不能把我背回去。

罗利并不喜欢这个建议，于是我不得不提醒他我们是最好的朋友，这就是好朋友为彼此做的事情之一。最后我主动提出帮他背书包，他总算让步了。

气喘吁吁呼哧

不过我有种预感，这桩买卖不会有第二次。罗利在我家门前卸下我时，已经筋疲力尽了。要是学校取消了我们放学的公交车，他们至少可以在我们家的山上安装一架缆车。

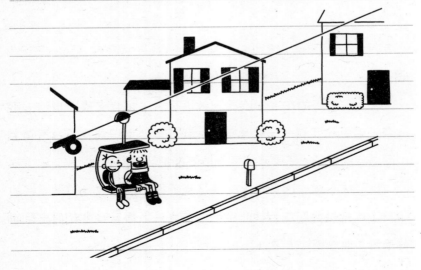

我已经就这个建议写了五封电子邮件给校长了，可我到现在还没收到一个字的回音。

　　到家的时候我也很累。我最新的变化是每天放学后要打个盹。

　　事实上，我是为睡觉而生的。放学后睡觉是唯一能让我恢复体力的办法。大多数时候，我一回到家，倒头便睡。

　　在睡觉方面我俨然是个专家。一旦我沉沉睡去，就能睡无止境。

　　我认识的人中唯一一个比我能睡的人是罗德里克，以下是我这样说的原因。几个星期前，老妈不得不给罗德里克订购一张新床，因为他已经把床睡坏了。家具店的工人把他的旧床垫和弹簧垫搬走了。

　　工人来的时候，罗德里克的放学觉睡到一半。他们抬走他的床垫时，他就睡在地上，躺在空荡荡的床框子中间。

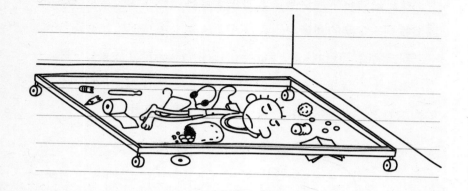

　　我担心这样下去老爸会禁止我们放学后睡觉。我开始感觉到，他烦透了每天晚上要叫醒我们俩起床吃饭。

周二

　　好吧，尽管我讨厌承认这个事实，但睡放学觉开始影响我的成绩了。

知道吧，以前我放学后一到家就做作业，到了晚上我就看电视。最近一段时间我在尝试边做作业边看电视，但有时候这不大行得通。

　　我今天要写一篇四页纸的生物论文，但昨晚我有点沉迷于我在看的节目。于是今天我不得不努力利用课余休息时间在电脑室写论文。

　　我没有太多时间做研究，就在页边距和字体大小上做文章，撑满四页纸。不过我敢说，诺兰太太肯定会找我麻烦的。

黑猩猩

四页纸的论文

作者：格雷·赫夫利

1

这是一只黑猩猩，简称"猩猩"。

猩猩是你拿在手上的这篇论文的研究对象。

2

42

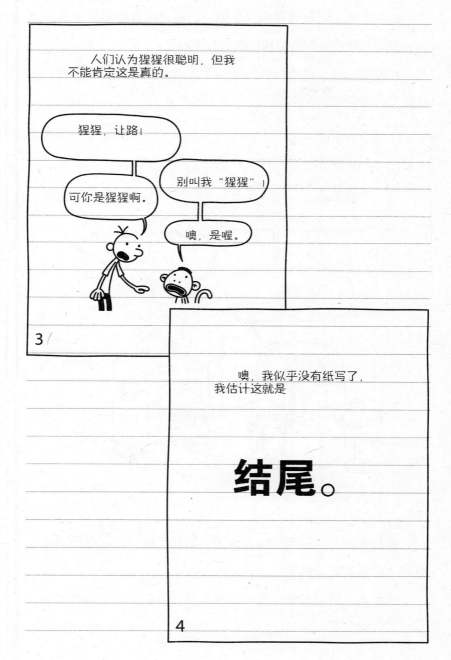

昨天地理小测我得了个"零蛋"。不过从我的角度来说，要同时复习考试内容和看足球比赛实在太难了。

老实跟你说，首先我认为老师不应该逼我们背这些东西，以后每个人都会有私人机器人，它会把你需要的任何知识告诉你。

提起老师，今天克雷格太太的心情糟糕透了。那是因为她放在桌上的大词典不见了。

我敢说，肯定是有人借了词典忘记归还，但克雷格太太一直用"偷"这个词。

　　克雷格太太说如果这节课下课前词典还没回到她的桌上，课间休息全部人都不许出教室。

　　然后她跟我们说她会离开教室，如果那个"罪犯"将词典完璧归赵，这件事就这么算了，她不会追究任何问题。

　　克雷格太太叫了帕蒂·法瑞尔做班长看管全班，然后就走了。帕蒂把班长的工作很当一回事，她管着我们的时候，没人敢越雷池半步。

我只是希望拿了词典的人赶快出来全盘招供，因为我午饭时只喝了两盒巧克力奶。

可没有人挺身而出。果不其然，克雷格太太兑现了她的承诺，课间不让我们离开教室。她说她每天课间都会让我们留在教室，直到词典还给她为止。

周五

过去三天克雷格太太都没让我们在课间出去，但词典还是没有现身。今天帕蒂·法瑞尔病了，于是克雷格太太让亚历克斯·阿鲁达负责在她离开时看管全班。

亚历克斯是个好学生，不过大家都不像害怕帕蒂·法瑞尔那样害怕他。克雷格太太一走，教室里就闹得天翻地覆。

亚历克斯·
阿鲁达

啪

几个受够了每天被禁闭在教室里的家伙决定调查一下是谁拿了克雷格太太的词典。

他们讯问的第一个人是这个叫柯瑞·兰姆的小孩。我觉得柯瑞之所以成为头号嫌疑人，是因为他聪明，说话又总是用大词。

柯瑞马上招认了他的罪行。不过事实表明，他说词典是他拿的，只是因为受审的压力太大，让他崩溃了。

名单的下一号是彼得·林恩，你还没反应过来他也已经招供了。

那些家伙早晚会找上门来，我知道得赶快想个办法。

神探夏洛克·萨米的书我看得多了，知道有时候得靠一个书呆子式的人出马才能从窘境中脱身。我觉得如果存在那个人，那个人准是亚历克斯·阿鲁达。

于是我和另外几个担心进入讯问名单的小孩去找亚历克斯，看他能不能让我们脱身。

我们告诉亚历克斯，我们需要他帮忙解开克雷格太太词典之谜，可他连我们在说什么都不知道。我猜亚历克斯对书如此沉迷，以致连过去几天身边发生了什么事都没有注意到。

　　而且，亚历克斯课间休息的时候总是坐在教室里看书，所以克雷格太太的惩罚对他的生活没有多少影响。

　　倒霉的是，亚历克斯也读过夏洛克·萨米的故事和他有关那部分，他说要是我们给他五块钱，他就帮我们。哼，这完全不公平嘛，因为夏洛克·萨米只收五分钱。不过我和其他人都一致认为这是物有所值的，于是我们几个人筹了五块钱，乖乖交给他。

　　我们把这件事巨细无遗地告诉亚历克斯，不过我们知道得不多。然后我们问亚历克斯能不能给我们指条明路。

　　我本来以为亚历克斯会记下要点，滔滔不绝地说些科学术语，但他只是合上自己读的书，给我们看封面。说来你也不信，那就是克雷格太太的词典。

　　亚历克斯说他这些天都在研读这本词典，准备下个月全州的拼字大赛。好吧，要是我们给他五块钱之前就知道这些情况，倒是不错的。不管怎么样，不能浪费时间抱怨了，因为克雷格太太随时可能回到教室里。

　　柯瑞·兰姆从亚历克斯手中一把夺过词典，放在克雷格太太的桌上。不巧就在那时她走进教室。

克雷格太太食言了，最后完全没有履行那个"不作追究"的诺言，接下来三个星期柯瑞•兰姆课间都得呆在教室里。不过往好的方面看，至少他有亚历克斯•阿鲁达作伴。

二月

周二

昨天在餐厅里，我把书包都清空了，也只找到两个水果——没有零食。

这是一个相当严重的问题。老妈总是往我的午餐包里放点曲奇饼或甜威化饼之类的零食，通常我只靠它们来填肚子。可今天……剩下的时间我一点力气都没有了。

一回到家，我就问老妈那两个水果是怎么一回事。她说她每回买的零食都够我们吃一个星期，所以一定是有人偷吃了洗衣间盒子里的零食。

我敢肯定老妈认定我就是那个偷零食的贼，可相信我，我以前已经受过教训了。

去年我从盒子里拿了零食，但我打开午餐袋拿出老妈的后备零食时，已经付出了代价。

今天午饭又是一模一样的东西：两个水果，没有零食。

就像我之前说的，我真的要靠那些糖分的能量才能振作精神。第六节上沃尔森先生的课时，我几乎睡着了，幸好我的头撞到自己的椅背，震醒了我。

一到家，我就向老妈抗议，别人吃了零食，遭殃的却是我，这不公平。可她说这周末她才会去商店购物，我得凑合着熬到那个时候。

找老爸也不管用。我对他抱怨一番，他只是提出要处罚被逮到的零食小偷，处罚措施是"不许敲鼓、不许打电玩一个星期"。很明显，他认为那个贼要么是我，要么是罗德里克。

我之前说过，不是我偷的，但我觉得老爸想到罗德里克是对的。趁罗德里克晚饭后走进浴室的时机，我下楼到他的房间去，看能不能发现些零食包装纸或者食物碎渣。

正当我在罗德里克房间里到处侦查的时候，我听见他下楼的脚步声。我得迅速藏起来，不知道为什么罗德里克一逮到我在他房间，就会气得面部扭曲不成人形，比如他昨天的反应。

就在罗德里克走到楼梯最后一级时，我蜷缩着躲进他书桌的柜子里，关上了门。罗德里克走进房里，扑通一下倒在床上，打电话给他的朋友沃德。

罗德里克和沃德谈个没完没了，我开始想我也许要在桌子里过夜。

罗德里克和沃德激烈地争论一个人倒立的时候会不会呕吐。我开始觉得自己快要吐了。所幸就在那时候，话筒的电池没电了。趁罗德里克上楼换话筒，我溜之大吉。

要是我有钱的话，这零食的事就不会是个问题。要是我有钱，我就可以每天到学校的自动售货机上买零食。

不过眼下，我有点穷。那是因为我把自己所有的零用钱都浪费在一些不能用的垃圾上。

大概一个月前，我在一本漫画书的封底上看到这些广告，我邮购了几件我以为会彻底改变自己生活的东西。

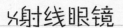

X射线眼镜

视线穿过:
墙壁·金属·衣服

个人气垫船

在一个垫子上周游
全城浮在地面上方
六英尺处用印钞机
打印你自己的钞票

插入一张白
纸，出来的
是5美元的票
子！

声音大挪移

腹语术①工具

两个星期前我陆续收到这些邮购的东西。

印钞机原来是个愚蠢的障眼把戏，你得把自己的钱放在机器
的密格里才能用。那还有什么意思，因为我真的指望这玩意能免
去我长大后的工作之苦。

X射线眼镜只会让你成为斗鸡眼，视线模糊。所以那也是竹篮
打水一场空。

① 懂得腹语术的人能用腹部发声，声音听起来像是从另一个人口中发出的。译者注

那个声音大挪移的东西压根用不了，尽管我已经照着使用说明手册来做了。

然而我期望值最高的东西是个人气垫船。我想等我的气垫船最后出现在信箱里，以后我放学回家就能快得像一阵风一样。

好吧，今天我终于收到那个包裹了，可里面没有气垫船。信里只有一张如何制造气垫船的方案，第一步我就没辙了。

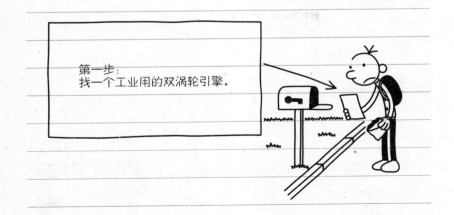

我真不能容忍那些广告商这样欺骗小·孩也可以逍遥法外。我考虑过聘请律师来起诉那些家伙，可请律师得花钱，要是有印钞机的话……正如我此前所说的，印钞机是件废物。

周四

　　今天，我放学后一到家，老妈已经在等着我。她看起来不大高兴。原来是学校往家里寄了期中成绩报告单，我还没来得及拦截她就已经收到信了。

　　老妈把报告单给我看，里面的内容有点难看。然后她说我们现在等老爸回家，看他怎么想。

　　天啊，再也没有比你惹上麻烦时等老爸回家更糟糕的事情了。以前我会躲在壁柜里，不过最近我找到一个更好的办法。现在，一旦我遇到麻烦，我就请奶奶过来吃晚饭，因为奶奶在的时候老爸不会对我发脾气。

晚饭时，我确保自己的位子紧挨着奶奶。

万幸的是老妈吃饭时没有提到我的报告单。奶奶一说她要去玩宾果游戏①，我马上跟着她出去了。

① 一个赢钱的游戏，每位玩家得到一张卡片，上面写有数字。工作人员随机叫号，若某位玩家卡片上的数字首先被全部叫出，则该名玩家获胜。译者注

　　我跟奶奶去玩宾果游戏不仅是为了躲开老爸，也是因为我需要一种十拿九稳的方法来赚点钱。

　　我盘算了一下，跟奶奶以及她的朋友玩几个小时宾果游戏，赢到的钱就够我在学校餐厅的自动售货机上买一个星期的零食了，相当划算。

　　奶奶和她的朋友都是宾果游戏专家，他们玩游戏也铆足了劲。他们有各种各样的辅助工具协助自己赢得游戏，比如说幸运记号和"宾果轮"等等。

　　奶奶有一个朋友可厉害了，她记得自己全部的牌，不需要用记号笔画道道。

　　不知为什么，今晚奶奶和她的朋友发挥失常，赢得不多。不过在玩"全部盖住①"的游戏时，我覆盖完所有格子。我不禁大喊一声："宾果"，一个工作人员过来检查我的牌。

① 随意抽取标有数码的小球，把玩家纸牌上的相应数码覆盖掉的一种游戏。译者注

事实证明是我弄错了，我覆盖了几个不应该被覆盖的方格。那个工作人员宣布我的胜利不算数，房间里其他人知道自己可以继续玩下去，都乐坏了。

奶奶提醒我，要是我再要喊"宾果"，别引起那么多人注意，因为这里的常客不喜欢看到一个新手赢。

我以为奶奶跟我开玩笑，不过话音刚落，那些老主顾就派出一位女士来恐吓我。我得承认，她的任务完成得相当漂亮。

周五

嗒，准确来说今天不是我过得最好的一天。首先，我挂了科学课考试。也许精明人的做法是昨天晚上复习功课而不是玩四个小时的宾果游戏。

今天上第六节课的时候我睡着了，这一次我睡得不省人事，直到沃森先生把我摇醒。我受到的处罚是坐在教室前面。

那正合我意，至少我在那里能睡个安稳觉。

我真希望第六节课下课后有人叫醒我，因为我一直到下一节课上课的时候才醒过来。

我醒过来的时候是罗瑞太太的课。她罚我留堂。下星期一放学后我还得呆在学校。

　　今天闹"糖荒"让我神经兮兮，可我没钱去便利店买汽水或糖果。于是我做了一件不大光彩的事。

　　我到罗利家，挖出我们埋在他家院里的时光宝盒。不过我是迫不得已才这么干的。

　　我把时光宝盒带回自己家，打开盒子，拿回我的三美元。然后我去便利店买了一大瓶汽水，一包小熊橡皮糖，还有一条糖块。

　　我有点感到难过，我和罗利凑份子的时光宝盒没能在地下呆几百年。另一方面，盒子被我们其中一个打开也是件好事，因为我们往盒里放的是一些确实很棒的东西。

周一

　　我真的不知道罚留堂是怎么样的。走入那个房间，我第一个念头是："我跟这些未来的罪犯不一样，我不属于这里。"

　　我坐在最后一张空椅子上，刚好坐在一个叫"里昂·瑞奇特"的小·孩前面。

　　里昂不是我们学校最聪明的孩子。他被罚留堂是因为他看到有只马蜂伏在教室的窗上，然后他就做了一件事。

　　我发现留堂的时候你要做的就是坐在那里，等待留堂时间结束。你不能读书或者做作业，什么事都不能做。这真是一个无聊的规定。这里的小·孩本来可以利用这额外的时间学习。

　　雷先生负责看管我们，他或多或少监视着我们的举动。不过每次雷先生在看别的地方的时候，里昂就会做拍一下我的耳朵，或者舔湿手指插入我的耳朵之类的事。最后里昂一时大意，被雷先生看到他的手指插在我的耳朵里。

　　雷先生说要是他再看到里昂碰我一下，里昂的麻烦就大了。

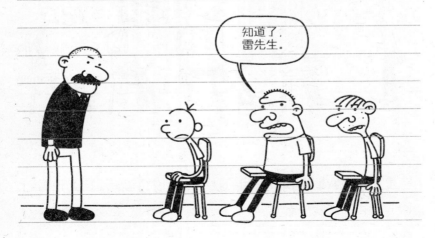

我知道里昂过不了一会又会来骚扰我，我打定主意要阻止他。雷先生的背一转过去，我就轻拍双掌一下，听起来就像是里昂在打我。

雷先生转过身来，对里昂宣布他要在这里多呆半小·时，明天他还得留堂。

回家路上，我一直在考虑我是不是做了有史以来在学校里最聪明的举动。我压根不是跑得最快的人，半小·时的领先优势并不大。

周二

　　今天晚上我意识到最近我的所有麻烦都拜家里的午餐零食大盗所赐，我下定决心要把他揪出来，一了百了。

　　我知道老妈周末刚去了杂货商店入货，洗衣间里有了一批新零食。那就是说零食大盗很有可能下手。

　　晚饭后我走进洗衣间里，关上灯。接着我爬进一个空的篮子里，守株待兔。

　　大概过了半小时，有人进来开了灯，不过那只是老妈。

　　老妈从干衣机里拿出衣服，我一动不动。老妈一点也没注意到篮子里的我，她径直把烘干的衣服扔进我藏身的篮子里。

　　然后她就走了，我还在等。我做了充分的心理准备在那里等一晚上，如果需要的话。

　　不过干衣机新鲜出炉的衣服真暖和，我开始觉得昏昏欲睡。我还没反应过来，就已经睡着了。

　　我不知道自己睡了多长时间，但我知道自己被玻璃纸发出的声音吵醒了。

我一听到嚼东西的声音，立马打开手电筒，当场把贼逮了个正着。

是老爸！天啊，我应该打一开始就想到他。说到垃圾食品，他完全是个瘾君子。

我正想开口狠狠教训老爸一顿，但他打断了我的话。他没兴趣和我谈他为什么要偷我们的午餐零食，他所关心的是我大半夜躲在一堆老妈的内衣内裤下面究竟在干什么。

就在那电光火石的一瞬间，我们听见老妈下楼的声音。

我想我和老爸都反应过来了，此刻我们两个说不清道不明的样子看起来有多么的狼狈。于是我们都大肆掠夺燕麦片，能拿多少就拿多少，然后逃之夭夭。

周三

　　我对老爸偷我们午餐零食的行径依然怒不可遏，打算今晚和他对质。但老爸六点就躺床上去了，我找不到机会。

　　老爸这么早就上床睡觉，是因为下班路上发生的一件事让他非常郁闷。

　　老爸在信箱取信，我们的邻居斯奈拉一家从街上走过来，推着他们的初生婴儿走下小山坡。

　　婴儿的名字叫塞思，我想他大概有两个月大。

　　每次斯奈拉夫妇生了小孩，六个月之后他们就会举行一个"半岁生日"的派对，邀请所有邻居参加。

每个斯奈拉的半岁生日派对的高潮，都是大人们排着队，施展十八般武艺逗婴儿笑。大人们做出各种各样傻里傻气的动作，让自己出尽洋相。

　　至今每个斯奈拉的半岁生日派对我都参加了，从来没有婴儿笑过一声。

咕咕咕咕咕！

　　大家都知道斯奈拉一家举行这些半岁生日派对的用心何在。赢得"美国最有趣的家庭"的一万美元大奖是他们的梦想。这个电视节目播放家庭拍摄的录像，比如有人的腹股沟被高尔夫球砸中诸如此类的东西。

　　斯奈拉一家一直希望派对上能出现令人捧腹大笑的事情，让他们用摄像机录下来。这些年来，他们确实拍了一些不错的东西。在萨姆·斯奈拉的半岁生日派对上，比特纳先生做立定跳远的时候裤子裂开了。在斯科特·斯奈拉的派对上，奥德姆先生倒着走的时候，摔进了婴儿游泳池里。

　　斯奈拉一家把那些录像带都寄给电视台了，但他们什么都没赢回来。我猜他们会一直生小孩，生到他们赢得奖项为止。

　　老爸恨透了当众表演，他会竭尽所能避免在一众邻居面前表现得像个傻子。到现在为止，老爸成功地逃开了斯奈拉家所有的半岁派对。

　　晚饭时，老妈通知老爸，他得出席塞思·斯奈拉六个月的半岁派对。我非常肯定老爸知道他大难临头了。

周四

　　学校的每个人最近都在议论下周就要到来的大型情人节舞会。

这是我们学校第一年举行舞会，人人都异常兴奋。班上有几个男生甚至已经邀请女生做他们的舞伴。

我和罗利眼下是单身汉，不过那不会妨碍我们华丽登场。

我考虑过，要是我和罗利接下来几天一起凑钱，我们可以在舞会当晚租一辆豪华轿车。我打电话给汽车公司，接电话那家伙竟然管我叫"夫人"。这一声称呼葬送了他拿到我这笔生意的机会。

舞会就在下周举行，我意识到自己得有套行头。

形势有点危急，我已经穿过圣诞节礼物中大部分的衣服，快没有干净衣服可穿了。我彻底翻查了一遍脏衣服，看看有没有可以穿第二次的。

摇啊
摇啊

我把要洗的衣服分成两堆：一堆是我可以再穿一次的，另一堆是穿在身上，就会被叫到鲍威尔护士的办公室听个人卫生讲座的。

闻一下

我在第一堆里找到一件看起来还好的衬衣，只不过左袖有块啫喱的污渍。所以到了舞会，我只需要记得让荷莉·希尔斯站在我的右边就好了。

情人节

昨晚我熬夜给班上每个人做情人节卡片。我敢肯定我的中学是全州唯一一间依然要求所有小孩互赠卡片的学校。

去年我打心里期待交换卡片。情人节前一夜，我花了不知多长时间，给我喜欢的女孩娜塔莎做了一张浪漫的卡片。

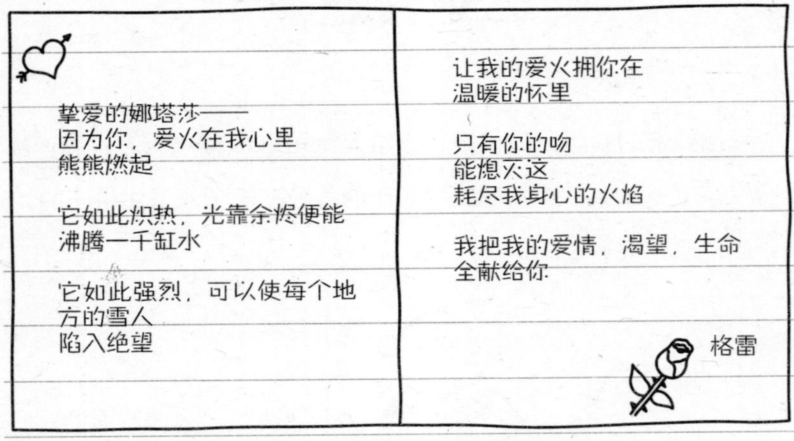

挚爱的娜塔莎——
因为你，爱火在我心里
熊熊燃起

它如此炽热，光靠余烬便能
沸腾一千缸水

它如此强烈，可以使每个地方的雪人
陷入绝望

让我的爱火拥你在
温暖的怀里

只有你的吻
能熄灭这
耗尽我身心的火焰

我把我的爱情，渴望，生命
全献给你

格雷

我把卡片给老妈看，让她给我检查有没有拼写错误，可她说我写的诗"不符合我的年龄"。她跟我说也许我该给娜塔莎一小盒糖果或者别的东西，不过我不打算从老妈身上获得什么恋爱建议。

学校里每个人都在教室里到处走，互相往对方的盒子里放情人节卡片，不过我是亲手将卡片交给娜塔莎的。

　　我让她读出卡片上的话，然后我等着看她送我什么。

　　娜塔莎翻遍她的盒子，抽出一张从商店里买回来的廉价卡片。这张卡片本来是给她的朋友仙黛儿的，不过她生病了。

　　娜塔莎画掉她朋友的名字，写上我的名字。

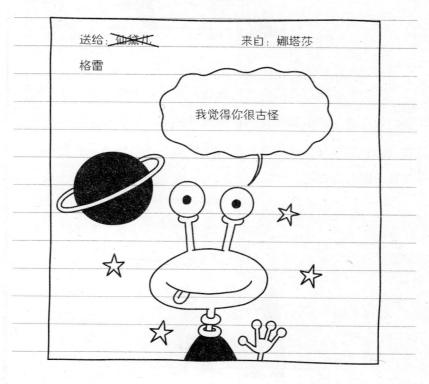

这下，你大概已经知道为什么今年我对交换卡片没有什么热情了吧。

昨晚我想到一个绝妙的点子。我知道我得给班上每个人做一张卡片，不过我不会做出一副感性的样子，写些言不由衷的话，我会把自己对他们的看法毫厘不差地告诉他们。

办法就是，我不在自己的卡片上签名。

好些个小孩向我们的老师瑞瑟太太告了卡片的状，她在教室里到处巡逻，想要找出发出这些卡片的人。我知道瑞瑟太太会认为没有收到那种卡片的人就是始作俑者，我已经为这种情况做好准备，因为我也给自己做了一张。

卡片交换完了便是情人节舞会。本来说舞会是在晚上，不过我估计他们没法找到那么多家长做义务陪护人。于是他们把舞会改在中午。

下午一点左右，老师们就开始让大家集合，领我们到体育馆。不想掏两美元入场费的人要到雷先生的房间里自习。不过对我们大部分人来讲，"自习"基本上就跟留堂一样。

其余的人排着队进了礼堂，坐在看台上。全部男生坐在礼堂一侧，女生坐在另一侧，这真是莫名其妙。等所有人都进了礼堂，老师们开始放音乐。可是选音乐的人也太落伍了吧，压根就不知道这些日子小孩听些什么音乐。

头十五分钟，没人动一下。然后我们的指导顾问菲利普先生和鲍威尔护士走到礼堂中央，跳起舞来。

我猜菲利普先生和鲍威尔护士以为要是他们领头跳舞，所有小孩就会跟着走下来，加入他们的行列。但是他们跳舞的真正效果是保证让所有人呆在自己的座位上。

最后，校长曼西太太，抓起扩音器，大声宣布，看台上的所有人都必须走下来跳舞，这将占我们体育课成绩的20%。

这时，我和几个男孩想偷偷溜去雷先生的房间，但我们被把守出口的老师抓住了。

曼西太太也没跟我们在体育成绩的事情上开玩笑。她和体育老师安德伍德先生到处走，后者手上拿着他的成绩登记册。

之前我已经快要挂掉体育课了，所以我知道这次要认真点。可我也不想自己在全班面前看起来像个傻瓜。于是我发明了我能做的最简单的能被称之为舞蹈的动作。

倒霉的是，一群同样担心体育成绩的男生看到我的动作，走到我身边来。紧接着，我被一群抄袭我舞步的白痴包围了。

我想躲开那些家伙，能躲多远就多远，于是我环顾体育馆，看看可以去哪里静静地跳舞。

这时，我瞥见了在房间对面的荷莉·希尔斯，我才记得自己大费周章来舞会图的是什么。

荷莉正和她的朋友在体育场中间跳舞，我跳着自己的步子舞，一点点靠近她们。

全部女孩围成一团，跳起舞来就像是职业舞蹈演员，大概是因为她们一旦有空就看MTV。

荷莉就在人群中间。我在圈子外围绕着跳了好一会，想找个入口，不过失败了。

到了最后，荷莉停了下来，去拿饮料喝，我知道这是天赐良机。

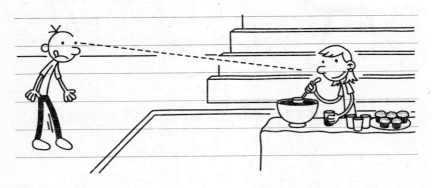

我正要朝荷莉走去，跟她说些俏皮话，可就在那节骨眼上，弗雷格不知从哪儿突然冒出来。

布吉布吉布吉！

弗雷格脸上盖满了粉红色的糖霜，大概他看到纸杯蛋糕被端到点心桌上时，整个人都发糖疯了。我敢打包票的是他完全报销了我和荷莉相处的机会，那本来会是一个美妙的时刻。

几分钟后，舞蹈结束了，我错过了给荷莉留下一个好印象的机会。放学后我独自一人步行回家，因为我需要一点时间一个人呆着。

晚饭后老妈告诉我信箱里有张情人节卡片，上面写着我的名字。我问她是谁寄来的，她只说是"一个特别的人"。我跑去信箱拿卡片，我得承认我的心情相当兴奋。我满心希望是荷莉给我的，不过我也不介意收到某些女孩的卡片，至少包括学校里那四五个女孩。

卡片装在一个粉红色的大信封里，我的姓名是用草书写着。我撕开信封口，发现了这些东西：一张彩色美术纸，上面贴了一块糖果。那是罗利寄的卡片。

有时候我真的搞不懂那家伙。

三月

周六

前一天老爸在沙发上发现曼尼的毯子"小·可爱"。我认为老爸并不知道那是什么，于是他把毯子扔掉了。

从那之后，曼尼孜孜不倦地翻遍整座房子找他的毯子，最后老爸不得不告诉曼尼是他不小心扔了"小·可爱"。嗜，曼尼昨天报仇雪恨了，他把老爸的内战战场模型当成游乐场。

曼尼也把气撒在所有人身上。今天我坐在沙发上想自己的事情时，曼尼走过来，朝我喊了一声——

① 原文ploopy 和 poop，poopy（均为儿语中大便的意思）发音类似，而且曼尼年幼，吐字不清。译者注

我不清楚"便便"是不是小·孩子骂人的脏话，但我不喜欢这个词的发音。于是我去找老妈，问她知不知道那是什么意思。

不幸的是，老妈正在聊电话，当她和朋友聊天时，你永远也无法引起她的注意。

我终于让老妈的嘴皮子停下一秒钟，但她因为我打断她聊天很不高兴。我告诉她曼尼喊我"便便"，然后她说——

我愣了一秒钟，因为我正要问她这个，看我没有回答，于是老妈回过头继续聊天。

那之后，曼尼知道，只要他愿意，随便什么时候叫我"便便"

都行，这就是他现在整天在做的事。

我觉得我应该知道打曼尼小报告不会给我带来任何好处。我和罗德里克还小的时候，我们经常到老妈那里告对方的状，老妈烦透了。于是她拿出一个叫告状乌龟的玩意儿来解决这个问题。

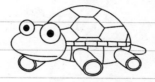

老妈以前教学前班的时候发明了告状乌龟这个玩意。告状乌龟的用途是，如果我和罗德里克闹矛盾，我们都别找老妈告状，找它去。喏，告状乌龟对罗德里克非常管用，可对我就不咋的。

TO TIM

DIARY
of a
Wimpy Kid

⑤

by Jeff Kinney

JANUARY

<u>New Year's Day</u>

You know how you're supposed to come up with a list of "resolutions" at the beginning of the year to try to make yourself a better person?

Well, the problem is, it's not easy for me to think of ways to improve myself, because I'm already pretty much one of the best people I know.

So this year my resolution is to try and help OTHER people improve. But the thing I'm finding out is that some people don't really appreciate it when you're trying to be helpful.

One thing I noticed right off the bat is that
the people in my family are doing a lousy job
sticking to THEIR New Year's resolutions.

Mom said she was gonna start going to the
gym today, but she spent the whole afternoon
watching TV.

And Dad said he was gonna go on a strict diet,
but after dinner I caught him out in the
garage, stuffing his face with brownies.

Even my little brother, Manny, couldn't stick-
with his resolution.

This morning he told everyone that he's a "big boy" and he's giving up his pacifier for good. Then he threw his favorite binkie in the trash.

Well, THAT New Year's resolution didn't even last a full MINUTE.

The only person in my family who didn't come up with a resolution is my older brother, Rodrick, and that's a pity because his list should be about a mile and a half long.

So I decided to come up with a program to help Rodrick be a better person. I called my plan "Three Strikes and You're Out." The basic idea was that every time I saw Rodrick messing up, I'd mark a little "X" on his chart.

Well, Rodrick got all three strikes before I even had a chance to decide what "You're Out" meant.

PUNCH
PUNCH
PUNCH

Anyway, I'm starting to wonder if I should just bag MY resolution, too. It's a lot of work, and so far I haven't really made any progress.

Besides, after I reminded Mom for like the billionth time to stop chewing her potato chips so loud, she made a really good point. She said, "Everyone can't be as perfect as YOU, Gregory." And from what I've seen so far, I think she's right.

96

Thursday

Dad is giving this diet thing another try, and that's bad news for me. He's gone about three days without eating any chocolate, and he's been SUPER cranky.

The other day, after Dad woke me up and told me to get ready for school, I accidentally fell back asleep. Believe me, that's the last time I'll make THAT mistake.

Part of the problem is that Dad always wakes me up before Mom's out of the shower, so I know that I still have like ten more minutes before I need to get out of bed for real.

Yesterday I came up with a pretty good way to get some extra sleep time without making Dad mad. After he woke me up, I took all of my blankets down the hall with me and waited outside the bathroom for my turn in the shower.

Then I lay down right on top of the heater vent. And when the furnace was blowing, the experience was even BETTER than being in bed.

The problem was, the heat only stayed on for about five minutes at a time. So when the furnace wasn't running, I was just lying there on this cold piece of metal.

This morning, while I was waiting for Mom to be done with her shower, I remembered someone gave her a bathrobe for Christmas. So I went into her closet and got it.

Let me just say that was one of the smartest moves I've ever made. Wearing that thing was like being wrapped in a big, fluffy towel that just came out of the dryer.

In fact, I liked it so much, I even wore it AFTER my shower. I think Dad might've been jealous HE didn't come up with the robe idea first, because when I came to the kitchen table, he seemed extra-grumpy.

MORNIN'!

I tell you, women have the right idea with this bathrobe thing. Now I'm wondering what ELSE I'm missing out on.

I just wish I had asked for my own bathrobe for Christmas, because I'm sure Mom is gonna make me give hers back.

I struck out on gifts again this year. I knew I was in for a rough day when I came downstairs on Christmas morning and the only presents in my stocking were a stick of deodorant and a "travel dictionary".

I guess once you're in middle school, grown-ups decide you're too old for toys or anything that's actually fun.

But then they still expect you to be all excited when you open the lame gifts they get you.

Most of my gifts this year were books or clothes. The closest thing I got to a toy was a present from Uncle Charlie.

When I unwrapped Uncle Charlie's gift, I didn't even know what it was supposed to be. It was this big plastic ring with a net attached to it.

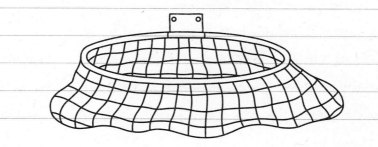

Uncle Charlie explained that it was a "Laundry Hoop" for my bedroom. He said I was supposed to hang the Laundry Hoop on the back of my door and it would make putting away my dirty clothes "fun".

At first I thought it was a joke, but then I realized Uncle Charlie was serious. So I had to explain to him that I don't actually DO my own laundry.

I told him I just throw my dirty clothes on the floor, and Mom picks them up and takes them downstairs to the laundry room.

Then a few days later, everything comes back to me in nice, folded piles.

I told Uncle Charlie he should just return the Laundry Hoop and give me cash so I could buy something I'd actually USE.

That's when Mom spoke up. She told Uncle Charlie she thought the Laundry Hoop was a GREAT idea.

Then she said that from now on I'd be doing my OWN laundry. So basically, it ends up that Uncle Charlie got me a chore for Christmas.

It really stinks that I got such crummy gifts this year. I put in a lot of effort buttering people up for the past few months, and I thought it would pay off on Christmas.

Now that I'm responsible for my own laundry, I guess I'm kind of GLAD I got a bunch of clothes. I might actually make it through the whole school year before I run out of clean stuff to wear.

Monday

When me and Rowley got to our bus stop today, we found a nasty surprise. There was a piece of paper taped to our street sign, and it said that, effective today, our bus route was "rezoned". And what that means is now we have to WALK to school.

Well, I'd like to talk to the genius who came up with THAT idea, because our street is almost a quarter of a mile from the school.

Me and Rowley had to run to make it to school on time today. And what REALLY stunk was when our regular bus passed us by and it was full of kids from Whirley Street, the neighborhood right next to ours.

The Whirley Street kids made monkey noises when they passed us, which was really annoying because that's exactly what WE used to do when we passed THEM.

I'll tell you one reason it's a bad idea to make kids walk to school. These days, teachers give you so much homework that, with all the books and papers you have to carry home, your backpack ends up weighing like a hundred pounds.

And if you want to see what kind of an effect that has on kids over time, all you have to do is look at Rodrick and some of his friends.

Instead of putting him right back to bed, Mom lets Manny sit with us and watch TV.

It's really not fair, because when Manny is with us, I'm not allowed to watch any of the shows I like.

All I can say is, when I was a kid there wasn't any of this "getting out of bed" stuff. I did it once or twice, but Dad put a stop to it real quick.

There was this book Dad used to read to me every night called "The Giving Tree". It was a really good book, but the back of it had a picture of the author, this guy named Shel Silverstein.

But Shel Silverstein looks more like a burglar or a pirate than a guy who should be writing books for kids.

Dad must have known that picture kind of freaked me out, because one night after I got out of bed, Dad said —

IF YOU GET OUT OF BED AGAIN TONIGHT, YOU'LL PROBABLY RUN INTO SHEL SILVERSTEIN IN THE HALLWAY.

That really did the trick. Ever since then, I STILL don't get out of bed at night, even if I really need to use the bathroom.

I don't think Mom and Dad read Manny any Shel Silverstein books, which probably explains why he keeps getting up after they put him to bed.

I've heard some of the stories Mom and Dad read to Manny, and let me just say that the people who write these books really have a racket going.

First of all, there are hardly any words in them, so I'm sure it only takes about five seconds to write one.

SILLY BEAR YAWNING,
SILLY BEAR SAD.

SILLY BEAR SLEEPING,
SILLY BEAR GLAD!

THE END.

I told Mom what I thought of Manny's books, and she said that if they were so easy to write, then I should try writing one myself.

So that's exactly what I did. Trust me, it wasn't hard, either. All you have to do is make up a character with a snappy name, and then make sure the character learns a lesson at the end of the book.

Now all I need to do is mail this thing off to a publisher and wait for the money to start rolling in.

Wise Up, Mr. Shropsharp!

by Greg Heffley

Once upon a time there was this man named Mr. Shropsharp who thought all these crazy thoughts.

One day Mr. Shropsharp took a ride in his car.

But then...

And then...

And so...

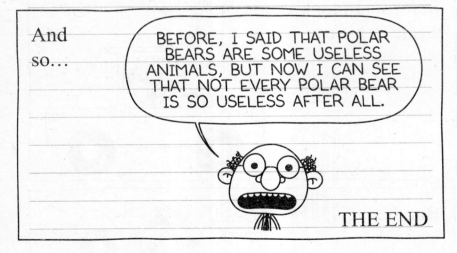

THE END

See what I mean? The only thing I noticed after I finished the book was that I forgot to make it rhyme. But the publisher is gonna have to pay me extra if they want THAT.

Saturday

Well, after spending the last two weeks walking to school, I was really looking forward to kicking back and doing nothing for two days.

The problem with watching TV on a Saturday is that the only thing that's on is bowling or golf. Plus, the sun comes through our sliding glass window, and you can barely see the TV screen anyway.

Today I wanted to change the channel, but the remote was on top of the coffee table. I was all comfortable, with my bowl of cereal in my lap, so I really didn't want to get up.

I tried using the Force to make the remote levitate to me, even though I've tried it a million times before and it's never worked once. Today I tried for about fifteen minutes and concentrated REALLY hard, but no luck. I just wish I'd known that Dad was standing right behind me the whole time.

Dad told me I was gonna have to go outside and get some exercise. I told Dad I exercise all the TIME and just this morning I used the bench press he got me.

But I should have come up with something more believable, because it was pretty obvious that wasn't true.

See, the reason Dad is on my case about exercise and all that is because he's got this boss named Mr. Warren, and Mr. Warren has three boys who are these crazy sports fanatics. Dad sees the Warren kids outside in their front lawn every day on his way home from work when his carpool goes by their house.

48...
49...
50!

So I think Dad is pretty disappointed every time he gets home and sees what HIS sons are up to.

Anyway, like I said, Dad kicked me out of the house today. I couldn't really think of anything I wanted to do, but then I had a good idea.

Yesterday at lunch, Albert Sandy was telling everyone about this guy in China or Thailand or someplace who could jump six feet straight up in the air, no joke. The way the guy did it was by digging a hole that was three inches deep and then jumping in and out of it a hundred times. The next day, the guy doubled the size of the hole, and he jumped in and out of THAT. By the fifth day, he was practically like a kangaroo.

118

Some of the guys at my table told Albert he was full of baloney, but what he was saying made a lot of sense to ME. Plus, I figured if I did what Albert said and then ADDED a few days to the program, all my problems with bullies could be over.

LOOKING FOR SOMEONE, FELLOWS?

I got a shovel out of the garage and found a place in the front yard that looked like a good spot to dig. But before I could even get started, Mom came outside and asked me what I was up to.

I told Mom I was just digging a hole, but of course she didn't like THAT idea. So she came up with about twenty reasons why I wasn't allowed to do it.

Mom told me it was "dangerous" to dig in the yard because of underground electrical lines and sewage pipes and stuff. Then she made me promise up and down that I wouldn't dig any holes in our yard. So I promised.

Mom went inside, but then she kept watching me out the window. I knew I was gonna have to take my shovel and go dig a hole somewhere else, so I headed up to Rowley's house.

I haven't been going up to Rowley's much lately, mostly because of Fregley. Fregley has been spending a lot of time in his front yard, and sure enough, that's where he was today.

My new strategy with Fregley is to just avoid eye contact and keep walking, and it seemed to do the trick today.

When I got to Rowley's, I told him my idea, and how the two of us would practically be ninjas if we stuck with this hole-jumping program I planned out.

But Rowley didn't seem so hot on the idea. He said his parents might get mad if we dug a ten-foot hole in his front yard without asking them, so he was gonna have to get their permission first.

Now, if there's one thing I know about Rowley's parents, it's that they NEVER like my ideas. I told Rowley we could just cover the hole up with a tarp or a blanket or something and put some leaves on top of it, and his folks would never even find out. That seemed to convince him.

122

OK, so I admit that Rowley's parents might EVENTUALLY find out. But that wouldn't be for at least three or four months.

Me and Rowley found a good spot in the front yard to start digging, but we ran into a problem right away.

The ground was pretty much frozen SOLID,
and we could hardly even make a dent.

I spent a few minutes trying before I handed
the shovel over to Rowley. He couldn't really
make any progress, either, but I gave him an
extra-long turn so he could feel like he was
contributing to the project.

Rowley got a little bit further than I did, but
when it started to get dark out, he gave up.

I guess we'll have to take another crack at this thing tomorrow.

Sunday
Well, I thought about it a lot overnight, and I realized that at the rate me and Rowley are going, we're gonna to be in college before this hole is ten feet deep.

So I came up with a totally DIFFERENT idea for what we could do. I remembered this thing I saw on TV where scientists made a "time capsule" and filled it with a bunch of stuff like newspapers and DVDs and things like that. Then the scientists buried their time capsule in the ground. The idea was that in a few hundred years someone will come along and dig it up, and they can learn how people from our time used to live.

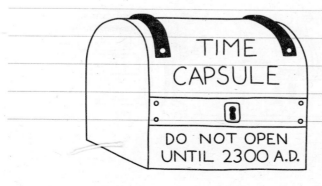

TIME CAPSULE

DO NOT OPEN UNTIL 2300 A.D.

I told Rowley about my idea, and he seemed pretty enthusiastic about it. Mostly, I think he was just glad we weren't gonna spend the next few years digging a hole.

I asked Rowley to donate some items to put in the time capsule, and that's when he got cold feet.

I told Rowley that if he put some of his Christmas presents in the time capsule, people in the future would get some really cool stuff when they opened the box. Rowley told me it wasn't fair, because I wasn't putting any of MY Christmas presents in the time capsule. So I had to explain to him that the people in the future would think we were really lame if they opened the box and it was filled with clothes and books.

Then I told Rowley I'd throw in three dollars of my OWN money to prove I was making sacrifices, too. That seemed to be enough to convince him to fork over one of his new video games and a couple of other things.

I actually had a secret plan that I wasn't letting Rowley in on. I knew that putting the cash in the time capsule was a smart move, because that money is gonna be worth a LOT more than $3.00 in the future.

So hopefully whoever finds the time capsule will travel back in time and reward me for making them rich.

I wrote a little note and put it in the box just to make sure the person who finds it knows exactly who to thank.

To whom it may concern:

The cash is from
Greg Heffley
12 Surrey Street

Me and Rowley found a shoe box and put all of our stuff in it. Then we sealed it up with some masking tape.

I wrote a little note on the outside of the box to make sure it didn't get opened too soon.

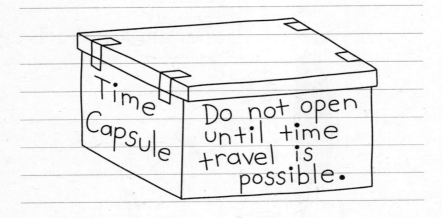

After that, we put it in the hole we dug yesterday and buried it as best we could.

I kind of wish Rowley had put some more effort into digging the hole, because our time capsule wasn't really buried all the way. Hopefully nobody will mess with it, because it needs to stay there for at least a few hundred years.

PAT
PAT

Monday
Well, my week got off to a rough start. When I got out of bed, Mom's bathrobe wasn't where it usually is, hanging on my doorknob.

I asked Mom if she took the robe back, but she said she didn't. So I have a feeling Dad had something to do with it.

A couple of days ago, I figured out a way to combine the bathrobe experience and the heating vent experience, and I don't think Dad really approved of my idea.

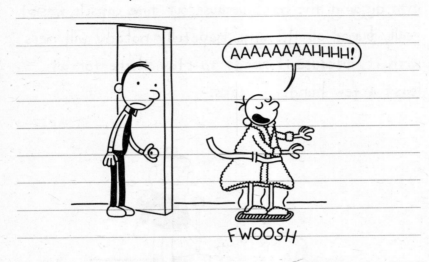

I figure he either hid the robe or got rid of it. Now that I think of it, Dad made a run to the Goodwill bin last night after dinner, so that's probably not a good sign.

Anyway, if Dad DID get rid of the robe, it wouldn't be the first time he's thrown out someone's personal property. You know how Manny has been trying to quit using his pacifier?

Yesterday morning Dad got rid of every single one of Manny's binkies.

Well, Manny totally freaked out. The only way Mom could get him to calm down was to dig out his old blanket, this thing he calls "Tingy."

Tingy started off as a blue blanket that Mom knitted for Manny's first birthday, and it was love at first sight.

Manny carried that thing around with him everywhere he went. He wouldn't even let Mom take it away from him so she could WASH it.

It started falling apart, and by the time Manny was two, his blanket was basically a couple of pieces of yarn held together by raisins and boogers.

I think that's when Manny started calling his
blanket "Tingy."

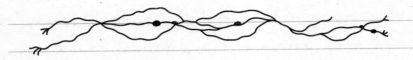

For the past couple of days, Manny's been
dragging Tingy around the house just like he
did when he was a baby, and I've been trying
to stay out of his way as much as possible.

Wednesday
I'm getting really tired of walking to school every
day, so this morning I asked Mom if she would
drive me and Rowley. The reason I didn't ask her
sooner is because Mom's car is covered in all these
embarrassing bumper stickers, and kids at my school
are brutal when it comes to that sort of thing.

I've tried scraping the bumper stickers off, but whatever kind of glue they put on those things is meant to last until the end of time.

Today me and Rowley got a ride from Mom, but I told her to let us out BEHIND the school.

Well, I made the dumb mistake of leaving my backpack in the car, so Mom brought it to me in fourth period. And of course she picked TODAY to finally start going to the gym.

It was just my luck, too. Fourth period is the only time I have a class with Holly Hills, and I've been trying to make a good impression on her this year. I figure this incident probably set me back about three weeks.

I'm not the only one who's trying to impress Holly Hills, either. I think just about every boy in my class has a crush on her.

Holly is the fourth-prettiest girl in the class, but the top three all have boyfriends. So a lot of guys like me are doing everything they can to get in good with her.

I've been trying to come up with an angle to separate myself from the rest of the goobers who like Holly. And I think I finally figured it out: humor.

See, the kids in my class are like Neanderthals when it comes to jokes. To give you an idea of what I'm talking about, here's the kind of thing that passes for comedy at my school —

Anytime Holly's in the area, I make sure I use my best material.

I've been using Rowley as my comedy partner, and I've actually trained him on a couple of pretty decent jokes.

The only problem is, Rowley's starting to get a little greedy about who gets to say what, so I don't know if this partnership is gonna work out long-term.

Friday

Well, I learned my lesson about getting a ride from Mom, so I'm back to walking to school. But when I was heading home with Rowley this afternoon, I seriously didn't think I had the energy to make it up the hill to my house. So I asked Rowley if he'd give me a piggyback ride.

Rowley didn't exactly jump at the idea, so I had to remind him that we're best friends and this is the kind of thing best friends do for each other. He finally caved when I offered to carry his backpack for him.

GASP
WHEEZE

I have a feeling this was a one-time thing, though, because Rowley was completely wiped out by the time he dropped me off at my house. You know, if the school is going to take away our bus ride home, the least they can do is install a ski lift on our hill.

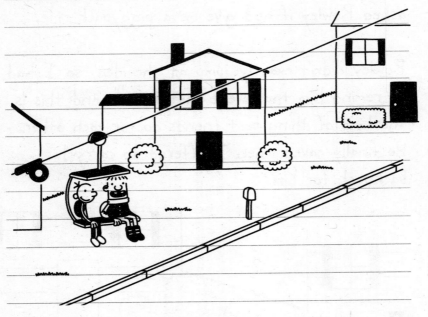

I've e-mailed the principal about five times with my suggestion, but I haven't heard anything back yet.

When I got to my house, I was pretty tired, too. My new thing is that I take a nap every day after school.

In fact, I LIVE for my naps. Sleeping after school is the only way I can really recharge my batteries, and on most days the second I get home, I'm in bed.

I'm actually kind of becoming an expert at sleeping. Once I'm out, I can sleep through just about anything.

The only person I know who's better at sleeping than me is RODRICK, and here's the reason I say that. A couple of weeks ago, Mom had to order Rodrick a new bed because he'd worn his out. So the furniture guys came to take his old mattress and box spring away.

When they came, Rodrick was in the middle of his after-school nap. So they took his bed away, and he just slept on the floor, right in the middle of his empty bed frame.

The thing I'm worried about is that Dad is going to ban our after-school naps. I'm starting to get the feeling he's sick of waking the two of us up for dinner every night.

Tuesday
Well, I hate to admit this, but I think my naps are starting to have an effect on my grades.

See, I used to do my homework when I got home from school, and then I watched TV at night. Lately I've been trying to do my homework WHILE I watch TV, and sometimes that doesn't work out too good.

I had this four-page Biology paper due today, but last night I kind of got caught up in this show I was watching. So I had to try to write the whole thing in the computer lab during recess today.

I didn't have a lot of time to do any research, so I played with the margins and the font size to stretch what I had to four pages. But I'm pretty sure Ms. Nolan is gonna call me on it.

CHIMPS

A four-page paper by

GREG
HEFFLEY

This is a
chimpanzee, or
"chimp" for short.

Chimps are the
subject of the paper
you're holding in your
hand right now.

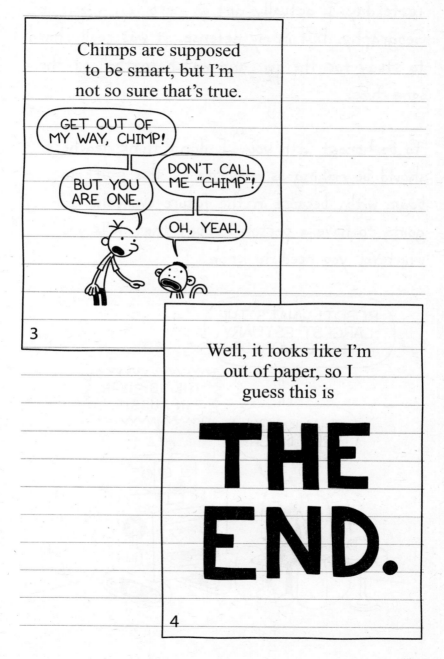

143

Yesterday I actually got a "zero" on a quiz in Geography. But in my defense, it was really hard to study for the quiz and watch football at the same time.

To be honest with you, I don't think teachers should be making us memorize all this stuff to begin with, because in the future everyone is going to have a personal robot that tells you whatever you need to know.

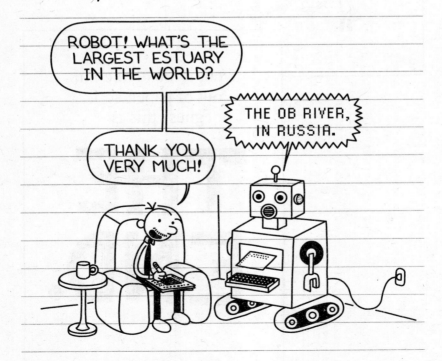

144

Speaking of teachers, today Mrs. Craig was in a really bad mood. That's because the big dictionary that usually sits on her desk was missing.

I'm sure someone just borrowed it and forgot to put it back, but the word Mrs. Craig kept using was "stole".

Mrs. Craig said that if the dictionary wasn't returned to her desk before the end of the period, she was keeping everyone inside for recess.

Then she told us she was going to leave the room, and that if the "culprit" returned the dictionary to her desk, there wouldn't be any consequences, and there would be no questions asked.

Mrs. Craig made Patty Farrell class monitor and left the room. Patty takes her job as class monitor really seriously, and when she's in charge, nobody dares to step out of line.

I was just hoping the person who took the dictionary would hurry up and come clean, because I had two cartons of chocolate milk for lunch.

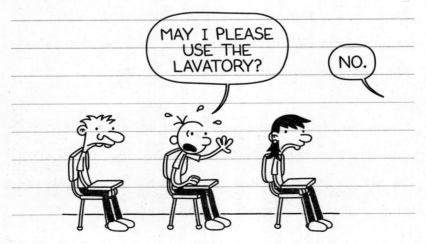

But nobody did come forward. And sure enough, Mrs. Craig stuck to her promise and kept us inside for recess. Then she said she was gonna keep us inside every day until the dictionary was returned.

Friday
Mrs. Craig has kept us inside for the past three days, and still no dictionary. Today Patty Farrell was sick, so Mrs. Craig put Alex Aruda in charge of the room while she was gone.

Alex is a good student, but people aren't afraid of Alex the way they are of Patty Farrell. As soon as Mrs. Craig left the room, it was complete pandemonium.

A couple of guys who were sick of getting stuck inside for recess every day decided to try and figure out who took Mrs. Craig's dictionary.

The first person they interrogated was this kid named Corey Lamb. I think Corey was number one on the list of suspects because he's smart and he's always using big words.

Corey fessed up to the crime in no time flat. But it turns out he only said he did it because the pressure made him crack.

SHAKE
SHAKE

SUCK
SUCK

The next kid on the list was Peter Lynn, and before you knew it Peter was confessing, too.

I figured it was just a matter of time before those guys cornered ME. So I knew I had to think up something fast.

I've read enough Sherlock Sammy books to know that sometimes it takes a nerd to get you out of a pinch. And I figured if anyone could crack this case, it was Alex Aruda.

So me and a couple of other guys who were worried about getting hassled went over to Alex to see if he could help us out.

We told Alex we needed him to solve the mystery of who took Mrs. Craig's dictionary, but he didn't even know what we were TALKING about. I guess Alex had been so wrapped up in his book that he hadn't even noticed what had been going on around him for the past couple of days.

Plus, Alex always stays inside to read during recess, so Mrs. Craig's punishment hadn't had a big effect on his life.

Unfortunately, Alex has read his share of Sherlock Sammy books, too, so he said he would help us if we paid him five bucks. Well, that was totally unfair, because Sherlock Sammy only charges a nickel. But me and the other guys agreed it was worth it, and we pooled our money, then forked over the five dollars.

We laid out all the facts of the case to Alex, but we didn't know a whole lot. Then we asked Alex if he could get us pointed in the right direction.

I expected Alex to start taking notes and spout some scientific mumbo jumbo, but all he did was close the book he was reading and show the cover to us. And you're not gonna BELIEVE this, but it was Mrs. Craig's dictionary.

Alex said he'd been studying the dictionary to get ready for the state spelling bee next month. Well, THAT would've been nice to know BEFORE we gave him our five bucks. Anyway, there was no time to waste complaining, because Mrs. Craig was gonna be back in the room at any second.

Corey Lamb grabbed the book from Alex and put it on Mrs. Craig's desk. But she walked in the room right at that moment.

Mrs. Craig ended up going back on her whole "no consequences" promise, so Corey Lamb is gonna be spending the next three weeks inside during recess. Looking on the bright side, though, at least he'll have Alex Aruda to keep him company.

FEBRUARY

Tuesday

Yesterday in the cafeteria, when I emptied out my lunch bag, I got TWO FRUITS—and no snacks.

This was a pretty big problem. Mom always packs cookies or sugar wafers or something in my lunch bag, and it's usually the only thing I eat. So I had no energy for the rest of the day.

When I got home, I asked Mom what the deal was with the two-fruits thing. She said she always buys enough treats to last us the whole week, so one of us boys must've taken the snacks out of the bin in the laundry room.

I'm sure Mom thinks I'm the one stealing the snacks, but believe me, I already learned my lesson about doing THAT.

Last year I took treats out of the bin, but I totally paid the price for it when I opened my lunch bag at school and pulled out Mom's substitute snack.

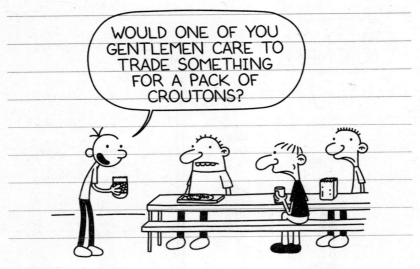

WOULD ONE OF YOU GENTLEMEN CARE TO TRADE SOMETHING FOR A PACK OF CROUTONS?

Today at lunch it was the same exact thing: two fruits and no snacks.

Like I said, I really depend on the boost I get from that sugar. I almost fell asleep in Mr. Watson's class in sixth period, but luckily I snapped awake when my head hit the back of my chair.

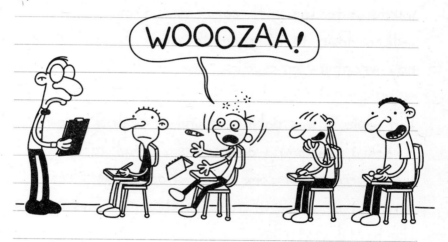

When I got home, I told Mom it wasn't fair someone else was eating the treats and I was having to suffer. But she said she wasn't going to go grocery shopping until the end of the week, and that I'd just have to "make do" until then.

Dad wasn't any help, either. When I complained to him, he just made up a penalty for anyone caught stealing snacks, which was "no drums and no video games for a week." So obviously he thinks it's either me or Rodrick.

Like I said, it's not ME, but I figured Dad might be right about Rodrick. When Rodrick went up to the bathroom after dinner, I walked down to his room to see if I could find any wrappers or crumbs.

But while I was poking around in Rodrick's room, I heard him coming downstairs. I had to hide quick, because for some reason Rodrick gets really bent out of shape when he catches me in his room, like he did yesterday.

Right before Rodrick got to the bottom of the stairs, I dove into his desk cabinet and shut the door. Rodrick walked in the room, then flopped on his bed and called his friend Ward.

Rodrick and Ward talked FOREVER, and I was starting to think I might have to spend the night in that desk.

Rodrick and Ward got into a pretty heated debate about whether or not a person could throw up while standing on their head, and I started to feel like I was gonna throw up myself. Luckily, right around then, the phone's battery died. When Rodrick went upstairs to get the spare phone, I made a run for it.

This snack thing wouldn't even be an issue if I had money. If I did, I could just buy something from the vending machine at school every day.

At the moment, though, I'm kind of broke. That's because I wasted all my money on some junk I can't even USE.

About a month ago, I saw these ads in the back of one of my comic books, and I sent away for a couple of things that were supposed to TOTALLY change my life.

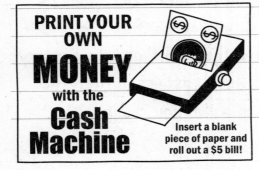

I started receiving my stuff in the mail about two weeks ago.

The Cash Machine turned out to be some stupid magic trick where you have to insert your OWN money in this secret slot for it to work. And that wasn't good, because I was really counting on that thing to get me out of having to find a job when I grow up.

The X-Ray Goggles just made you see blurry and cross-eyed, so that was a bust, too.

OOF!

The Throw Your Voice thing didn't work at ALL, even though I followed the instructions in the book.

But the item I had the highest hopes for was the Personal Hovercraft. I figured getting home after school would be a breeze once my hovercraft finally showed up in the mail.

Well, I got the package today, but there wasn't a hovercraft inside. There was just a blueprint for how to BUILD a hovercraft, and I got stuck on Step One.

<u>Step One</u>:

Acquire an industrial twin-turbine engine.

I just can't believe the people who write those ads can get away with lying to kids like that. I thought about hiring a lawyer to sue those guys, but lawyers cost money, and like I said before, the Cash Machine was a piece of garbage.

Thursday
Today, when I got home from school, Mom was waiting for me, and she didn't look too happy. It turns out the school sent home mid-quarter report cards, and she got the mail before I could intercept it.

Mom showed me the report card, and it wasn't pretty. Then she said we were gonna wait for DAD to get home to see what HE thought.

Man, waiting for Dad to get home when you're in trouble is the WORST. I used to just hide in the closet, but recently I figured out a better way to handle it. Now, whenever I get in trouble, I ask Gramma to come over for dinner, because Dad's not gonna act mad at me if Gramma's around.

At dinner, I made sure I sat in the seat right next to Gramma.

Luckily, Mom didn't mention my report card during dinner. And when Gramma said she needed to leave to go to Bingo, I tagged right along with her.

CATCH YOU GUYS LATER!

Escaping Dad wasn't the ONLY reason I went to Bingo with Gramma. I also went because I needed a surefire way to make some money.

I figured spending a few hours with Gramma and her Bingo friends was a pretty fair price to pay for a week's worth of snacks from the vending machine in the school cafeteria.

Gramma and her friends are EXPERTS at Bingo, and they're real serious about it, too. They have all sorts of gear like lucky blotters and "Bingo Trolls" and stuff like that to help them win.

One of Gramma's friends is so good that she memorizes all her cards, and she doesn't even NEED to use a blotter to mark them off.

For some reason, tonight Gramma and her friends weren't winning like they usually do. But then on the "Cover All" game, I got every square. I yelled out "BINGO" real loud, and the clerk came over to check my card.

It turns out I messed up and covered a couple of squares that I shouldn't have. The clerk announced that my win was no good, and everyone else in the room was pretty happy that they could keep playing.

Gramma told me not to call so much attention to myself if I called out "Bingo" again, because the regulars don't like it when a newcomer wins.

I thought Gramma was pulling my leg, but sure enough, the regulars sent one of their ladies over to intimidate me. And I have to admit, she did her job really well.

Friday
Well, today wasn't exactly my best day ever. For starters, I flunked my Science test. So it probably would've been a good idea to have studied last night instead of spending four hours at Bingo.

I fell asleep in sixth period today, and this time I was out COLD—Mr. Watson had to shake me to get me to wake up. As a punishment, I had to sit in the front of the room.

That was just fine with me, because at least up there I could sleep in peace.

I just wish someone woke me up when sixth period ended, because I didn't wake up until the NEXT period started.

The class I woke up in was taught by Mrs. Lowry.
Mrs. Lowry gave me detention, and on Monday
I'm gonna have to stay after school to serve it.

Tonight I was totally jittery from my sugar
withdrawal, but I didn't have any money to go
buy a soda or candy from the convenience store.
So I did something I'm not real proud of.

I went to Rowley's and dug up the time capsule we
buried in his front yard. But I only did it because
I was desperate.

I took the time capsule back to my house, opened
it up, and got out my three bucks. Then I went
down to the convenience store and bought myself a
big soda, a pack of gummy bears, and a candy bar.

I guess I feel a little bad that the time capsule me and Rowley put together didn't stay buried for a few hundred years. On the other hand, it's kind of neat that one of US got to open it, because we had actually put some really good stuff in there.

Monday

I didn't really know what to expect from detention, but when I walked into the room, the first thought I had was, "I don't belong in here with these future criminals."

I took the only empty seat, which was right in front of this kid named Leon Ricket.

Leon is not the brightest kid in our school. He was in detention because of what he did when a wasp landed on the window in homeroom.

I found out that all you do in detention is sit there and wait for it to be over. You're not allowed to read or do your homework or ANYTHING, which is a pretty dumb rule, considering that most of the kids in there could really use the extra study time.

Mr. Ray was the moderator, and he more or less kept an eye on us. But every time Mr. Ray looked away, Leon would flick my ear or give me a Wet Willie or something like that. Eventually Leon got careless, and Mr. Ray caught Leon with his finger in my ear.

Mr. Ray said if he caught Leon touching me again, he was gonna be in BIG trouble.

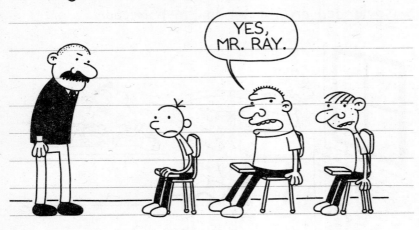

I knew Leon was just gonna go back to bugging me, so I decided to put a stop to it. As soon as Mr. Ray's back was turned, I slapped my hands together to make it seem like Leon hit me.

Mr. Ray turned around and told Leon he was gonna have to stay another half hour, and that he had detention again TOMORROW.

On the way home, I was wondering if I made the smartest move back there at the school. I'm not exactly the fastest runner, and a half hour isn't that big of a head start.

Tuesday
Tonight I realized ALL of my current problems can be traced back to when someone in my family started stealing the lunch snacks. So I decided to catch the thief once and for all.

I knew Mom had gone grocery shopping over the weekend, so there was a fresh supply of snacks in the laundry room. That meant the snack thief was pretty much guaranteed to strike.

After dinner I went in the laundry room and turned off the light. Then I climbed in an empty basket and waited.

About a half hour later, someone came in the room and turned on the light, so I hid under a towel. But it turns out it was just Mom.

I stayed perfectly still while she got clothes out of the dryer. Mom didn't notice me in there, and she dumped the clothes from the dryer right into the bin where I was hiding.

DUMP

Then she walked out of the room, and I waited some more. I was seriously ready to wait there all night if that's what it took.

But the clothes from the dryer were really warm, and I started feeling a little drowsy. And before I knew it, I was asleep.

ZZZZZ

I don't know how many hours I slept, but what I DO know is that I woke up to the sound of crinkling cellophane.

When I heard the sound of chewing, I turned on my flashlight and caught the thief red-handed.

It was Dad! Man, I should have known it was him from the start. When it comes to junk food, he's a total ADDICT.

I started to give Dad a piece of my mind, but he cut me off. He wasn't interested in talking about why he was stealing our lunch snacks. What he WAS interested in talking about was what the heck I was doing buried in a pile of Mom's underwear in the middle of the night.

Right at that moment, we heard Mom coming down the stairs.

I think me and Dad realized how bad the situation looked for both of us, so we each just grabbed as many oatmeal creams as we could carry and made a run for it.

Wednesday
I was still really steamed at Dad for stealing our lunch treats, and I was planning on confronting him tonight. But Dad was in bed by 6:00, so I didn't get my chance.

Dad went to bed so early because he was depressed about something that happened when he got home from work. When Dad was getting the mail, our neighbors from up the street, the Snellas, walked down the hill with their new baby.

HEY THERE, FRANK!

The baby's name is Seth, and I think he's about two months old.

Every time the Snellas have a baby, six months later they throw a big "half-birthday" party and invite all the neighbors.

The highlight of each Snella half-birthday party is when the adults line up and try to make the baby laugh. The grown-ups do all these wacky things and make COMPLETE fools of themselves.

GOO GOO GOO GOO GOO!

I've been to every single Snella half-birthday party so far, and no baby has laughed once.

Everyone knows the REAL reason the Snellas have these half-birthday parties is because their big dream is to win the $10,000 Grand Prize on "America's Funniest Families." That's this TV show where they play home movies of people getting hit in the groin with golf balls and stuff like that.

The Snellas are just hoping something really funny will happen at one of their parties so they can catch it on videotape. They've actually gotten some pretty good stuff over the years. During Sam Snella's half-birthday party, Mr. Bittner split his pants doing jumping jacks. And during Scott Snella's party, Mr. Odom was walking backward, and he fell in the baby pool.

WWAAUUGH!

WHIRR

The Snellas turned in those videos, but they didn't win anything. So I guess they're just gonna keep having babies until they do.

Dad HATES performing in front of people, so he'll do everything he can to avoid having to act like a fool in front of the whole neighborhood. And so far, Dad has weaseled his way out of every single Snella half-birthday party.

At dinner, Mom told Dad he HAS to go to Seth Snella's half-birthday party in June. And I'm pretty sure Dad knows that this time, his number is finally up.

Thursday
Everybody at school has been talking about the big Valentine's Dance that's coming up next week.

This is the first year at my school that they've actually had a dance, so everyone's all excited. Some of the guys in my class were even asking girls if they would be their dates to the dance.

Me and Rowley are both bachelors at the moment, but that's not gonna stop us from arriving in style.

I figured if me and Rowley scraped together some money in the next few days, we could rent a limo for the night. But when I called the limo company, the guy who answered the phone called me "Ma'am." So that pretty much blew any chance he had of getting MY business.

Since the dance is next week, I realized I was gonna need something to wear.

I'm kind of in a pinch because I've already worn most of the clothes I got for Christmas, and I'm almost out of clean stuff to wear. I went through my dirty clothes to see if there was anything I could wear a SECOND time.

I separated my laundry into two piles: one that I could wear again, and one that would get me sent down to Nurse Powell's office for a lecture on hygiene.

I found a shirt in pile number one that wasn't so bad, except it had a jelly stain on the left-hand side. So at the dance, I'll just need to remember to keep Holly Hills to the right of me at all times.

Valentine's Day

I was up late last night making Valentine's cards for everyone in my class. I'm pretty sure my middle school is the only one in the state that still makes all the kids give cards to one another.

Last year I was actually looking forward to the card swap. The night before Valentine's Day, I spent a lot of time making an awesome card for this girl named Natasha who I kind of liked.

Beloved Natasha —

For you, a fire blazes in my heart

So strong that the embers alone could bring a thousand hot tubs to a boil

So intense that it causes snowmen everywhere to despair

Let the bonfire of my love wrap you in its warmth

Only your kiss could quench the flames that so consume me

To you I pledge my love, my desire, my life

Greg

I showed Mom my card to check for spelling errors, but she said what I wrote wasn't "age appropriate." She told me maybe I should just get Natasha a little box of candy or something, but I wasn't about to take romantic advice from my mother.

At school everyone went around the room and put their Valentine's cards in one another's boxes, but I delivered my card to Natasha personally.

I let her read it, and then I waited to see what she made for ME.

Natasha dug around in her box and pulled out this cheap store-bought card that was supposed to be for her friend Chantelle, who was out sick that day.

Then Natasha scribbled out her friend's name and put MY name on it instead.

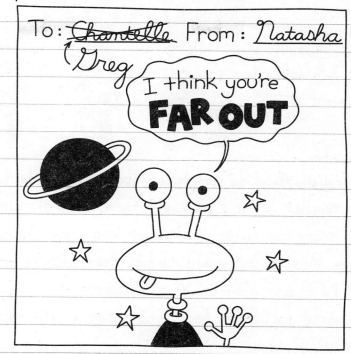

To: ~~Chantelle~~ ↑Greg From: Natasha

I think you're FAR OUT

Anyway, you can probably see why I wasn't too enthusiastic about the card exchange THIS year.

Last night I came up with a great idea. I knew I had to make a card for everyone in the class, but instead of being all mushy and saying things I didn't really mean, I told everyone EXACTLY what I thought of them.

The trick was, I didn't actually SIGN any of my cards.

A few of the kids complained about the cards to our teacher, Mrs. Riser, and then she went around the room trying to figure out who sent them. I knew Mrs. Riser would think that whoever DIDN'T get a card was the culprit, but I was prepared for that, because I made a card for MYSELF, too.

After the card exchange came the Valentine's Dance. The dance was originally supposed to be at NIGHT, but I guess they couldn't get enough parents to volunteer to be chaperones. So they put the dance smack in the middle of the school day instead.

The teachers started rounding everyone up and sending them down to the auditorium at around 1:00. Anyone who didn't want to cough up the two bucks for admission had to go down to Mr. Ray's room for study hall.

But it was pretty obvious to most of us that "study hall" was basically the same thing as detention.

The rest of us filed into the gym and sat in the bleachers. I don't know why, but all the boys sat on one side of the gym, and all the girls sat on the other. Once everyone was inside the gym, the teachers started the music. But whoever picked out the songs is SERIOUSLY out of touch with what kids are listening to these days.

YOU DO THE HOKEY POKEY AND YOU TURN YOURSELF AROUND...

For the first fifteen minutes or so, no one moved a muscle. Then Mr. Phillips, the guidance counselor, and Nurse Powell walked to the middle of the gym and started dancing.

I guess Mr. Phillips and Nurse Powell thought if THEY started dancing, all the kids would come down onto the floor and join them. All they REALLY did was GUARANTEE that everyone stayed in their seat.

Finally, Mrs. Mancy, the principal, grabbed a microphone and made an announcement. She said that everyone in the bleachers was REQUIRED to come down onto the floor and dance, and it would count for 20% of our Phys Ed grades.

At that point me and a couple of other boys tried to sneak out to go down to Mr. Ray's room, but we got caught by some teachers who were blocking the exits.

Mrs. Mancy wasn't kidding about the gym grade thing, either. She was walking around with Mr. Underwood, the Phys Ed teacher, and he was carrying his gradebook with him.

I'm already close to flunking Phys Ed, so I knew it was time to get serious. But I didn't want to look like a fool in front of the kids in my class, either. So I just came up with the simplest move I could do that would technically qualify as "dancing."

Unfortunately, a bunch of guys who were worried about THEIR Phys Ed grades saw what I was doing, and they came over to where I was. And the next thing I knew, I was surrounded by a bunch of bozos who were stealing my moves.

I wanted to get as far away from those guys as I could, so I looked around the gym for a place where I could go and dance in peace.

That's when I spotted Holly Hills across the room, and I remembered why I even bothered coming to the dance in the first place.

Holly was dancing with her friends in the middle of the gym, and I started doing my step-dance thing, moving slowly toward them.

All the girls were lumped together in one big pack, and they were dancing like professionals, probably because they spend all their free time watching MTV.

Holly was right in the middle of the group. I kind of danced around the outside of the circle for a while, trying to find an opening, but I couldn't.

Finally, Holly stopped dancing and went to get a drink, and I knew it was my big chance.

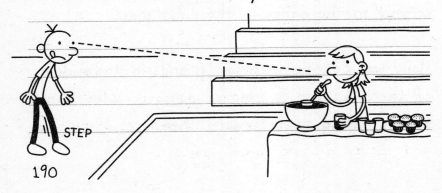

STEP

But just when I was about to go up to Holly and say something witty, Fregley came flying in out of NOWHERE.

BOOGIE BOOGIE BOOGIE!

Fregley had pink frosting covering his face, so he was probably all hopped-up on sugar from the cupcakes they were serving at the refreshments table. All I know for sure is that he TOTALLY ruined what should have been a great moment between me and Holly.

A few minutes later, the dance was over, and I missed my chance to make a good impression on her. I walked home alone after school, because I just needed a little time by myself.

191

After dinner Mom told me there was a Valentine's card out in the mailbox with my name on it. When I asked her who it was from, she just said, "someone special." I ran out to the mailbox and got the card, and I have to admit I was pretty excited. I was hoping it was from Holly, but there are at least four or five other girls at my school who I wouldn't mind getting a card from, either.

The card was in a big pink envelope with my name written in cursive. I ripped it open, and here's what I found: a sheet of construction paper with a piece of candy taped to it, and it was from ROWLEY.

Sometimes I just don't know about that boy.

MARCH

<u>Saturday</u>
The other day Dad found Manny's blanket, Tingy, on the couch. I don't think Dad knew what it was, so he threw it away.

Ever since then Manny's been turning the house upside down looking for his blanket, and finally Dad had to tell him that he accidentally threw it out. Well, Manny got his revenge yesterday by using Dad's Civil War battlefield as a playset.

Manny's been taking his anger out on everyone else, too. Today I was sitting on the couch just minding my own business, and Manny walked up to me and said —

I didn't know if "Ploopy" was some kind of little-kid bad word or what, but I didn't like the sound of it. So I went to find Mom and ask her if SHE knew what it meant.

Unfortunately, Mom was on the phone, and when she's gabbing with one of her friends, it takes forever to get her attention.

I finally got Mom to stop talking for a second, but she was mad that I interrupted her. I told her Manny called me "Ploopy," and she said —

That kind of threw me for a second, because it's the exact question I was trying to ask HER. I didn't have an answer, so Mom just went back to her conversation.

After that, Manny knew he had a green light to call me Ploopy whenever he wanted, and that's what he's been doing all day.

I guess I should've known that telling on Manny wasn't gonna get me anywhere. When me and Rodrick were little, we used to tell on each other so much that it made Mom crazy. So she brought out this thing called the Tattle Turtle to solve the problem.

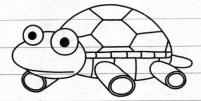

Mom came up with the Tattle Turtle idea when she taught preschool. The idea behind the Tattle Turtle was that if me and Rodrick had a problem with each other, we had to tell the Tattle Turtle instead of Mom. Well, the Tattle Turtle worked out GREAT for Rodrick, but not so much for me.

TATTLE TURTLE, RODRICK STOLE ALL THE MONEY FROM MY PIGGY BANK!

ACKNOWLEDGMENTS

Thanks to my wife, Julie, without whose love and support these books would not be possible. Thanks to my family—Mom, Dad, Re, Scott, and Pat—and to my extended family—the Kinneys, Cullinanes, Johnsons, Fitchs, Kennedys, and Burdetts. You have all been so supportive of this endeavor, and it has been great fun to share this experience with you!

Thanks, as always, to my editor, Charlie Kochman, for taking a chance on this series; to Jason Wells, the best publicity director in the business; and to all of the great folks at Abrams.

Thanks to my boss, Jess Brallier, and to all of my coworkers at Family Education Network.

Thanks to Riley, Sylvie, Carla, Nina, Brad, Elizabeth, and Keith out in Hollywoodland.

Thanks to Mel Odom for his wonderfully bombastic write-ups of the first two books.

And thanks to Aaron Nicodemus for encouraging me Way Back When to pick up my cartooning pen after I had given up.

ABOUT THE AUTHOR

Jeff Kinney is the creator of Poptropica.com, and the author of the #1 *New York Times* bestsellers *Diary of a Wimpy Kid* and *Diary of a Wimpy Kid: Rodrick Rules*, as well as the *Diary of a Wimpy Kid Do-It-Yourself Book*. He spent his childhood in the Washington D.C. area and moved to New England in 1995. Jeff lives in southern Massachusetts with his wife, Julie, and their two sons, Will and Grant.

望子快乐

朱子庆

　　在一个人的一生中，"与有荣焉"的机会或有，但肯定不多。因为儿子译了一部畅销书，而老爸被邀涂鸦几句，像这样的与荣，我想，即使放眼天下，也没有几人领得吧。

　　儿子接活儿翻译《小屁孩日记》时，还在读着大三。这是安安他第一次领译书稿，多少有点紧张和兴奋吧，起初他每译几段，便飞鸽传书，不一会儿人也跟过来，在我面前"项庄舞剑"地问："有意思么？有意思么？"怎么当时我就没有作乐不可支状呢？于今想来，我竟很有些后悔。对于一个喂饱段子与小品的中国人，若说还有什么洋幽默能令我们"绝倒"，难！不过，当安安译成杀青之时，图文并茂，我得以从头到尾再读一遍，我得说，这部书岂止有意思呢，读了它使我有一种冲动，假如时间可以倒流，我很想尝试重新做一回父亲！我不免窃想，安安在译它的时候，不知会怎样腹诽我这个老爸呢！

　　我宁愿儿子是书里那个小屁孩！

　　你可能会说，你别是在做秀吧，小屁孩格雷将来能出息成个什么样子，实在还很难说……这个质疑，典型地出诸一个中国人之口，出之于为父母的中国人之口。望子成龙，一定要孩子出息成个什么样子，虽说初衷也是为了孩子，但最终却是苦了孩子。"生年不满百，常怀千岁忧。"现在，由于这深重的忧患，我们已经把成功学启示的模式都做到胎教了！而望子快乐，有谁想过？从小就快乐，快乐一生？惭愧，我也是看了《小屁孩日记》才想到这点，然而儿子已不再年少！我觉得很有些对不住儿子！

我从来没有对安安的"少年老成"感到过有什么不妥，毕竟少年老成使人放心。而今读其译作而被触动，此心才为之不安起来。我在想，比起美国的小屁孩格雷和他的同学们，我们中国的小屁孩们是不是活得不很小屁孩？是不是普遍地过于负重、乏乐和少年老成？而当他们将来长大，娶妻（嫁夫）生子（女），为人父母，会不会还要循此逻辑再造下一代？想想安安少年时，起早贪黑地读书、写作业，小四眼，十足一个书呆子，类似格雷那样的调皮、贪玩、小有恶搞、缰绳牢笼不住地敢于尝试和行动主义……太缺少了。印象中，安安最突出的一次，也就是读小学三年级时，做了一回带头大哥，拔了校园里所有自行车的气门芯并四处派发，仅此而已吧（此处请在家长指导下阅读）。

说点别的吧。中国作家写的儿童文学作品，很少能引发成年读者的阅读兴趣。安徒生童话之所以风靡天下，在于它征服了成年读者。在我看来，《小屁孩日记》也属于成人少年兼宜的读物，可以父子同修！谁没有年少轻狂？谁没有豆蔻年华？只不过呢，对于为父母者，阅读它，会使你由会心一笑而再笑，继以感慨系之，进而不免有所自省，对照和检讨一下自己和孩子的关系，以及在某些类似事情的处理上，自己是否欠妥？等等。它虽系成人所作，书中对孩子心性的把握，却准确传神；虽非心理学著作，对了解孩子的心理和行为，也不无参悟和启示。品学兼优和顽劣不学的孩子毕竟是少数，小屁孩格雷是"中间人物"的一个玲珑典型，着实招人怜爱——在格雷身上，有着我们彼此都难免有的各样小心思、小算计、小毛病，就好像阿Q，读来透着与我们有那么一种割不断的血缘关系，这，也许就是此书在美国乃至全球都特别畅销的原因吧！

最后我想申明的是，第一读者身份在我是弥足珍惜的，因为，宝贝儿子出生时，第一眼看见他的是医生，老爸都摊不上第一读者呢！

我眼中的 ……

好书，爱不释手！

　　★　王汐子（女，19岁，2009年留学美国，攻读大学传媒专业）《小屁孩日记》在美国掀起的阅读风潮可不是盖的，在我留学美国的这一年中，不止一次目睹这套书对太平洋彼岸人民的巨大影响。高速公路上巨大的广告宣传牌就不用说了，我甚至在学校书店买课本时看到了这套书被大大咧咧地摆上书架，"小屁孩"的搞笑日记就这样理直气壮地充当起了美国大学生的课本教材！为什么这套书如此受欢迎？为什么一个普普通通的小男孩能让这么多成年人捧腹大笑？也许可以套用一个万能句式："每个人心中都有一个XXX"。每个人心中都有一个小屁孩，每个人小时候也有过这样的时光，每天都有点鸡毛蒜皮的小烦恼，像是作业这么多怎么办啦，要考试了书都没有看怎么办啦……但是大部分时候还是因为调皮捣乱被妈妈教训……就这样迷迷糊糊地走过了"小屁孩"时光，等长大后和朋友们讨论后才恍然大悟，随即不禁感慨，原来那时候我们都一样呀……是呀，全世界的小屁孩都一样！

　　★　读者 书山有径（发表于 2010-01-31）这是一本真正写给孩子的书。作为圣诞礼物买给女儿，由于作业多，平时只能睡前读几页。放假了，女儿天天捧着这本书，一天到晚为书的人和事笑个不停；天天给我讲鬼屋的故事，用神秘而恐怖的语气。并且，天天问我，生活中她的朋友哪些应该被叫做"小屁孩"，怎么个"屁"法。

★ 读者 zhizhimother（发表于 2009 – 06 – 12）在杂志上看到这书的介绍，一时冲动在当当上下了单，没想到，一买回来一家人抢着看，笑得前仰后翻。我跟女儿一人抢到一本，老公很不满意，他嘟囔着下一本出的时候他要第一个看。看多了面孔雷同的好孩子的书，看到这本，真是深有感触，我们的孩子其实都是这样长大的～～

轻松阅读 捧腹大笑

★ 这是著名的畅销书作家小巫的儿子 Sam 口述的英语和中文读后感：I like *Diary of a Wimpy Kid* because Greg is an average child just like us. His words are really funny and the illustrations are hilarious. His stories are eventful and most of them involve silliness. 我喜欢《小屁孩日记》，因为 Greg 是跟我们一样的普通孩子。他的故事很好玩儿，令我捧腹大笑，他做的事情很搞笑，有点儿傻呵呵的。书里的插图也很幽默。

★ 读者 bnulizi（发表于 2009 – 06 – 08）同学在开心网里转帖推荐这套书，于是我便傻傻地买了一套。看后发现还是挺赞的，笑料很多啊。而且最精彩的地方往往都是通过一段文字后的那幅图来表达的，我笑到肚子痛……

★ 读者 dearm 暖 baby（发表于 2009 – 07 – 29）我 12 岁了，过生日时妈妈给我买了这样两本书，真的很有趣！一半是中文，一半是英文，彻底打破了"英文看不懂看下面中文"的局限！而且这本书彻底地给我来了次大放松，"重点中学"的压力也一扫而光！总之，两个字：超赞！

★ 读者 mei298（发表于 2010 – 01 – 23）儿子超喜欢，边看边

大笑。买了1~4册，没几天就看完了，特别喜欢那一段"弗雷格跟我在同一个班上体育课，他的语言自成一家，比如说他要去厕所的时候，他就说——果汁！果汁！！！我们已经大致清楚弗雷格那套了，不过我看老师们大概还没弄懂。老师说——好吧，小伙子……你可真难侍候！还端来了一杯汽水。"为了这段话，儿子笑了一整天，到睡觉的时候想想还笑。

孩子爱上写日记了！

★　读者 pinganfurong（发表于 2009 - 11 - 10）一直想让九岁的儿子记记日记，但始终不喜欢给他"布置任务"。生活啦、工作啦、学习啦、休闲啦、娱乐啦等等等等，都是自己的事，自己喜欢，才能做好。写文章、记日记，也是如此。给老师写，为爹妈记，是件很烦人的事。命题作文、任务日记，只会让孩子讨厌写作文，讨厌记日记。讨厌的事能干好？笑话！怎么办呢？怎样才能让儿子自觉自愿地喜欢上记日记呢？于是，给儿子买了《小屁孩日记》。果不其然，儿子读完后，便拉着我去给他买回一个又大又厚的日记本，兴趣盎然地记起日记来。

★　读者 ddian2003（发表于 2009 - 12 - 22）正是于丹的那几句话吸引我买下了这套书。自己倒没看，但女儿却用了三天学校的课余时间就看完了，随后她大受启发，连着几天都写了日记。现在这书暂时搁在书柜里，已和女儿约定，等她学了英文后再来看一遍，当然要看书里的英文版本了。所以这书还是买得物有所值的。毕竟女儿喜欢！！

做个"不听话的好孩子"

★　读者 水真爽（发表于 2010 - 03 - 27）这套书是买给我上小

学二年级的儿子的。有时候他因为到该读书的时间而被要求从网游下来很恼火。尽管带着气，甚至眼泪，可是读起这本书来，总是能被书中小屁孩的种种淘气出格行为和想法弄得哈哈大笑。书中的卡通漫画也非常不错。这种文字漫画形式的日记非常具有趣味性，老少咸宜。对低年级孩子或爱画漫画的孩子尤其有启发作用。更重要的是提醒家长们好好留意观察这些"不怎么听话"的小屁孩们的内心世界，他们的健康成长需要成人的呵护引导，但千万不要把他们都变成只会"听大人话"的好孩子。

★ 读者 寂寞朱丽叶（发表于 2009 - 06 - 10）最近我身边的朋友都在看这本书，出于好奇我也买了一套，美国"囧男孩"格雷满脑子的鬼主意，虽然不是人们心目中好孩子的形象，但很真实，我很喜欢他，还有点羡慕他，我怎么没有他有趣呢。

对照《小屁孩日记》分享育儿体验

★ 读者 gjrzj2002@＊＊＊.＊＊＊（发表于 2010 - 05 - 21）看完四册书，我想着自己虽然不可能有三个孩子，但一个孩子的成长经历至今仍记忆犹新。儿子还是幼儿的时候，比较像曼尼，在爸妈眼中少有缺点，真是让人越看越爱，要什么就基本上能得到什么。整个幼儿期父母对孩子肯定大过否定。上了小学，儿子的境地就不怎么从容了，上学的压力时时处处在影响着他，小家伙要承受各方面的压力，父母、老师、同学，太过我行我素、大而化之都是行不通的，比如没写作业的话，老师、家长的批评和提醒是少不了的，孩子在慢慢学着适应这种生活，烦恼也随之而来，这一阶段比较像格雷，虽然儿子的思维还没那么丰富，快乐和烦恼的花样都没那么多，但处境差不多，表扬和赞美不像以前那样轻易就能得到了。儿子青年时代会是什么样子我还不得而知，也不可想象，那种水到渠成的阶段要靠前面的积累，我希望自己到时候能平心静气，坦然接受，无论儿子成长成什么样子。

　　亲爱的读者，你看完这本书后，有什么感想吗？请来电话或是登录本书的博客与我们分享吧！等本书再版时，这里也许换上了你的读后感呢！

　　我们的电话号码是020－83795744，博客地址是：blog. sina. com. cn/wimpykid。

悦读"小·屁孩"

《小·屁孩日记①——鬼屋创意》

在日记里，格雷记叙了他如何驾驭充满冒险的中学生活，如何巧妙逃脱学校歌唱比赛，最重要的是如何不让任何人发现他的秘密。他经常想捉弄人反被人捉弄；他常常想做好事却弄巧成拙；他屡屡身陷尴尬境遇竟逢"凶"化吉。他不是好孩子，也不是坏孩子，就只是普通的孩子；他有点自私，但重要关头也会挺身而出保护朋友……

《小·屁孩日记②——谁动了千年奶酪》

在《小·屁孩日记②》里，主人公格雷度过一个没有任何奇迹发生的圣诞节。为打发漫长无聊的下雪天，他和死党罗利雄心勃勃地想要堆出"世界上最大的雪人"，却因为惹怒老爸，雪人被销毁；格雷可是不甘寂寞的，没几天，他又找到乐子了，在送幼儿园小朋友过街的时候，他制造了一起"虫子事件"吓唬小朋友，并嫁祸罗利，从而导致一场"严重"的友情危机……格雷能顺利化解危机，重新赢得好朋友罗利的信任吗？

《小·屁孩日记③——好孩子不撒谎》

在本册里，格雷开始了他的暑假生活。慢着，别以为他的假期会轻松愉快。其实他整个暑

假都被游泳训练班给毁了。他还自作聪明地导演了一出把同学齐拉格当成隐形人的闹剧，他以为神不知鬼不觉就可以每天偷吃姜饼，终于在圣诞前夜东窗事发，付出了巨大的代价……

《小·屁孩日记④——偷鸡不成蚀把米》

本集里，格雷仿佛落入了他哥哥罗德里克的魔掌中一般，怎么也逃脱不了厄运：他在老妈的威逼利诱下跟罗德里克学爵士鼓，却只能在一旁干看罗德里克自娱自乐；与好友罗利一起偷看罗德里克窝藏的鬼片，却不幸玩过火害罗利受伤，为此格雷不得不付出惨重代价——代替罗利在全校晚会上表演魔术——而他的全部表演内容就是为一个一年级小朋友递魔术道具。更大的悲剧还在后面，他不惜花"重金"购买罗德里克的旧作业想要蒙混过关，却不幸买到一份不及格的作业。最后，他暑假误入女厕所的囧事还被罗德里克在全校大肆宣扬……格雷还有脸在学校混吗？他的日记还能继续下去吗？

《小·屁孩日记⑤——午餐零食大盗》

格雷在新的一年里展开了他的学校生活：克雷格老师的词典不翼而飞，于是每天课间休息时所有同学都被禁止外出，直至字典被找到；格雷的午餐零食从糖果变成了两个水果，他怀疑是哥哥罗德里克偷了零食，誓要查出真相。因为午餐零食闹的"糖荒"，让格雷精神不振，总是在下午的课堂上打瞌睡。格雷没有多余的零用钱，不能自己买糖果，于是他想到了自己埋下的时光宝盒——里面放着三美元的钞票。格雷挖出时光宝盒，暂时缓解了"糖荒"。另一边厢，学校即将举行第一次的情人节舞会。格雷对漂亮的同班同学荷莉心仪已久，就决定趁舞会好好表现。在舞会上，他成功与荷莉互相交换了情人节卡片，并想邀请荷莉跳舞，于是他向人群中的荷莉走去……

《小·屁孩日记⑥——可怕的炮兵学校》

格雷想尽一切办法让老爸摆脱一些可怕的念头。格雷的老爸一直希望他能加强锻炼，就让他加入了周末的足球队。格雷在足球队吃尽了苦头：他先被教练派去当球童，在荆棘丛里捡球累了个半死；然后又被要求坐在寒风中观赛，冷得他直打哆嗦；后来他自以为聪明地选择了后备守门员的位置，最后却因为正选守门员受伤而不得不披挂上阵。在输掉足球比赛后，格雷觉得老爸因此而生气了。未想老爸又冒出另一个更可怕的念头：把格雷送进炮兵学校。格雷却自动请缨加入周末的童子军，因为这样一来他就不必再去参加足球训练了。然而，在童子军的父子营中，格雷又为老爸惹来麻烦……老爸决定在这个学期结束后，就立刻把格雷送进炮兵学校。眼看暑假就要开始了，格雷因此坐立不安……

《小·屁孩日记⑦——从天而降的巨债》

暑假刚开始，格雷就与老爸老妈展开了拉锯战：老爸老妈坚持认为孩子放暑假就应该到户外去活动，但格雷却宁愿躲在家里打游戏

机、看肥皂剧。不得已之下，格雷跟着死党罗利到乡村俱乐部玩，两人在那儿吃了一点东西，就欠下了83美元的"巨债"。于是，他们不得不想尽一切办法打工还债……

他们能把债务还清吗？格雷又惹出了什么笑话？

《小屁孩日记⑧——"头盖骨摇晃机"的幸存者》

老妈带全家上了旅行车，看到防晒霜和泳衣，格雷满心以为是去海滩度假，却原来只是去水上乐园——一个令格雷吃过很多苦头的地方，过去的不愉快记忆也就罢了，这次好不容易做好一切准备，广播却通知"因闪电天气停止营业"；回到家里又怎样呢？格雷发现他心爱的鱼惨遭罗德里克宠物鱼的"毒口"；盼望已久的小狗阿甜来了，非但不是补偿，反而使格雷的生活一团糟；格雷发现救生员是希尔斯小姐，这使得他一改对于小镇游泳场的糟糕看法，小心眼儿活动起来；妈妈安排了一个格雷与爸爸改善关系的机会，可是格雷却用"甲壳虫小姐"召来了警察，搞得老爸灰溜溜的，他们关系更僵；老妈处心积虑安排格雷和死党罗利的一家去了海滩，格雷却又惹了祸……

我们可爱又倒霉的格雷啊，他该如何处理这一切？"头盖骨摇晃机"又是怎么回事？